THE BLACK MOUNTAIN
LEGEND OF HEADLESS ANNIE

THE BLACK MOUNTAIN LEGEND OF HEADLESS ANNIE

HENSLEY

CONTENTS

The True Story of Headless Annie on Black Mountain

*T*he Black Mountain Legend
   Of Headless Annie
By
DOUG HENSLEY
Copyright @ Doug Hensley 2024
AUTHOR'S NOTES

This book is dedicated to my good friend, Scottie Hall, who came from Harlan, Kentucky and had heard the stories Of Headless Annie and the Curse of Black Mountain. He stated his Father even had an encounter with Headless Annie. Scottie said his Father told him she jumped up on the hood of his car as he drove the lonely road of Black Mountain but he barely escaped her as the fog rolled in after him. Scottie, nor his siblings were ever allowed on Black Mountain. I want to thank Scottie for telling me this story that some say is only a legend. But is it?

.For decades, the ghost of **Headless Annie** has haunted the winding, fog-covered roads of **Black Mountain** in Harlan, Kentucky. Locals speak of a woman dressed in white, her head missing, who appears on dark, misty nights to those unfortunate enough to cross her path. The stories, passed down through generations, are chillingly consistent: a headless figure emerging from the shadows, her presence felt long before she is seen, and the sudden disappearance of those who encounter her.

The legend began with a tragic tale—Annie, a young woman, was said to have lost her life in a

violent accident on the treacherous mountain roads. But death was only the beginning. Ever since, drivers have reported seeing her spectral figure in their headlights just before they lose control of their vehicles, their cars inexplicably stalling, or hearing strange sounds in the thick mountain fog. Witnesses describe the overwhelming feeling of dread, the icy chill in the air, and the unmistakable sense that they are not alone.

Many have gone missing after encountering Headless Annie. One chilling tale recounts a couple who vanished without a trace, leaving their car abandoned, its doors open wide. Another incident involved a truck driver who was found in his cab, with a single bloodstained glove as the only clue to his disappearance. Even in recent years, a group of teenagers who sought to prove the legend false disappeared, with only a cellphone left behind, its last message an unfinished warning: "She's here..."

This book, "Headless Annie: The Curse of Black Mountain," is a work of fiction, but it draws inspiration from numerous real-life accounts of those who claim to have encountered Headless Annie. Their stories are eerie and inexplicable, filled with strange coincidences and mysterious disappearances.

Some call it folklore; others swear it is the truth.

Are you brave enough to explore the legend? Dive into the chilling pages of this novel, and experience the terror of Headless Annie for

yourself—but be warned, not everyone who ventures up Black Mountain comes back.

TABLE OF CONTENTS

The Haunting Begins

A group of friends arrives in Harlan, Kentucky, where they hear the local legend of Headless Annie. Despite warnings, they decide to explore the haunted Black Mountain.

The First Encounter

The friends have their first terrifying encounter with Annie, who appears out of the fog, headless and malevolent. They barely escape but are left deeply shaken.

The History of Black Mountain

The group delves into the dark history of Black Mountain and the story of Headless Annie, uncovering details about her tragic death and the many disappearances connected to her spirit.

Uncovering Secrets

Strange occurrences intensify as the group investigates deeper, discovering a hidden journal with clues to Annie's torment and the true extent of the curse that binds her.

The Abandoned Cabin

The group finds an old cabin in the woods where Annie was reportedly last seen alive. Inside, they discover disturbing evidence that suggests a more sinister force at work.

Annie's Warning

A séance goes horribly wrong, and the group receives a cryptic warning from Annie herself. They realize they must understand her pain to break the curse, but they also sense a darker presence watching them.

Divided by Fear

Tensions rise as fear and paranoia grip the group. Doubts and divisions threaten their unity, making them more vulnerable to Annie's malevolent influence.

The Descent into Darkness

The group ventures deeper into the forest, experiencing a series of terrifying encounters that test their resolve and sanity. One of them begins to see visions of Annie's life and death.

The Forgotten Grave

Following the clues in the journal, the group locates Annie's unmarked grave. They attempt to perform a ritual to put her spirit to rest but are interrupted by a malevolent force.

A Shattered Alliance

Disagreements turn violent, leading to a splintering of the group. The fog returns,
thickening around them as a powerful storm hits the mountain, trapping them.

Voices in the Fog

Lost in the fog, they hear whispers calling their names. One by one, they confront their darkest fears, realizing the mountain itself is alive with the spirits of the lost.

The Reckoning

The group reunites at a cliff's edge, where they face a horrific manifestation of Annie's suffering. They are forced to confront their own guilt and secrets to survive.

A Desperate Bargain

Realizing they have misinterpreted the ritual, they negotiate with Annie's spirit, but she is unwilling to rest until they understand the full truth of her death.

The Midnight Chase

A frantic chase through the woods ensues as the group is pursued by something far more terrifying than Annie—a dark entity that Annie herself seems afraid of.

The Cryptic Journal

They decode the final entries in the journal, uncovering a chilling revelation about the true nature of Annie's curse and the dark force that controls the mountain.

The Forgotten Ritual

The group attempts an ancient and
forbidden ritual to cleanse the mountain, but something goes wrong. The forest reacts violently, trapping them in a nightmarish loop.

Betrayed by Shadows

One member of the group betrays the others, thinking it will save them. This act unleashes an even greater evil, turning the forest into a living nightmare.

Confronting the Dark Entity

With no other choice, the survivors confront the dark entity that has been controlling the mountain and holding Annie's spirit captive for decades.

Breaking the Curse

The final showdown takes place on a stormy cliff side, where the group battles the entity and attempts to free Annie's spirit once and for all.

1. **A New Beginning... or an Old End?** They succeed in releasing Annie, but as they leave the mountain, they realize the curse has changed, evolving into something new—hinting that the darkness is not yet defeated and may one day return

CHAPTER 1: THE LEGEND OF HEADLESS ANNIE

Part 1: The Setting and the Atmosphere

The chapter opens with a scene in a dimly lit, creaky old museum in Lynch, Kentucky. The walls are lined with faded photographs of coal miners and early settlers, with a small section dedicated to local legends and folklore. The air is thick with dust, and the smell of old books lingers. A storm rages outside, adding a sense of foreboding with flashes of lightning illuminating the darkened room.

The museum's curator, **Henry Calloway**, an elderly man in his late seventies with a voice cracked from years of storytelling, is in the middle of a guided tour for a group of tourists. He's known for his captivating way of telling local legends, but tonight there's a different energy. He seems more hesitant, almost as if he's reluctant to tell this particular story.

As he speaks, he gazes at a black-and-white photograph on the wall — a blurry image of a woman in white standing on a fog-covered mountain road. The photograph is labeled "The Last Sighting of Headless Annie – 1952." The tourists lean in, intrigued and slightly nervous.

Henry begins to recount the story, his voice low and gravelly. He tells them about the chilling legend of Headless Annie, the ghost who haunts the winding roads of Black Mountain, appearing in the thick of the fog, searching for something — or someone.

Part 2: Henry's Haunting Past

As Henry speaks, his eyes occasionally flicker with fear. Unbeknownst to the tourists, Henry has a personal connection to the legend. Years ago, when he was a young boy, his older sister, **Martha Calloway**, vanished on Black Mountain. The authorities chalked it up to a runaway case, but Henry never believed it. He knew his sister too well — she was courageous, the kind who faced things head-on. He remembers the day she disappeared like it was yesterday. It was a foggy evening, and Martha had gone to the mountain to prove that the ghost stories were just tales. She never returned.

Haunted by her disappearance, Henry devoted his life to uncovering the truth. His fear is palpable — he has spent years piecing together bits of information, listening to those who claim to have seen Annie, and reading every scrap of paper related to the ghost stories. But he knows he is still missing something, some vital clue that might explain everything.

Part 3: Introducing the Tourists

Among the group of tourists are four main characters whose backgrounds and personal struggles will become integral to the unfolding story.

1. **Claire Morgan**: A young journalist in her early thirties from New York, Claire has come to Lynch to write an article about small-town legends. She is skeptical of ghost stories, seeing them as nothing more than local folklore used to entertain or scare people. She's ambitious, driven by a desire to uncover the truth and make a name for herself. But beneath her tough exterior, she harbors a deep-seated fear of the unknown

— a fear that stems from her childhood when her father, a police officer, went missing under mysterious circumstances. She never got closure, and it's a wound that hasn't healed.

1. **Eddie Lee**: A retired truck driver in his sixties, Eddie has returned to Lynch after spending most of his life on the road. He's a grizzled man with a gruff demeanor and a no-nonsense attitude, but his tough exterior hides a softer side. His wife died years ago, and he's been searching for something ever since. Eddie has a particular fear of Black Mountain; his father was the truck driver who disappeared there in the 1970s. Eddie grew up hearing the stories, and now he's back, determined to face his fear and find

out what really happened to his dad.

1. **Rachel Thompson**: A local high school teacher in her late forties, Rachel is known for her passion for history and folklore. She's deeply superstitious and believes in the paranormal. Rachel's grandmother used to tell her stories of Headless Annie, and those stories terrified her as a child. Now, she's convinced that Annie's spirit is restless and that something terrible is about to happen. She's been having nightmares about the ghost, and she feels an inexplicable pull to the mountain, like she's being called there.
2. **Derek Sullivan**: A twenty-five-year-old adventure enthusiast and YouTuber, Derek is in Lynch to film a

documentary about the town's ghost stories. He's a thrill-seeker, always looking for the next adrenaline rush. He doesn't believe in ghosts; to him, everything has a logical explanation. But he's hiding a secret — he has a crippling fear of being alone in the dark, a fear that stems from a childhood trauma he's never spoken about. He brushes it off as silly, but the fear is very real to him.

Part 4: The Legend Takes Shape

As Henry continues his story, he delves into the various sightings of Headless Annie over the years,

describing each incident in vivid detail. The tourists listen with a mix of fascination and skepticism, but Henry's voice grows more intense, more urgent. He recounts the story of the young couple in the 1950s, their car stalling in the fog, and the man disappearing without a trace. He speaks of the blood-stained glove found in the abandoned truck, and the teenagers who vanished after taunting the ghost with their bravado.

Henry's descriptions are terrifyingly vivid — the sound of a soft, eerie humming in the fog, the feeling of being watched, the cold that seeps into your bones, and the paralyzing fear that grips you when you see her, headless, in her flowing white dress, her hands outstretched as if reaching for something — or someone.

The tourists begin to shift uncomfortably. Claire remains skeptical, but she's intrigued by the emotional weight of Henry's words. Rachel is visibly shaken, her hands trembling.

Eddie looks stoic, but his eyes are haunted by the mention of the truck driver. Derek smirks, but there's a hint of unease in his expression.

Then, a young man among the tourists, **Sam Harris**, a local college student, nervously raises his hand and shares a story of his own. He talks about how, a week ago, his cousin claimed to have seen a woman in white on the mountain while driving home. The cousin hasn't been the same since, suffering from nightmares and refusing to talk about what he saw.

Part 5: The Uninvited Guest

As the tension builds, a loud crash is heard outside the museum. The group startles, and the lights flicker. Henry pauses, his face paling. The door creaks open, and a drenched man stumbles in. He is **Tom Mitchell**, a local hunter known for his solitude and eccentric behavior. His clothes are soaked, and his eyes are wide with fear.

Tom, panting, claims to have just come from Black Mountain. He swears he saw a figure in white moving through the fog and heard a soft, mournful humming that seemed to be coming from all directions at once. His dog ran away, and he barely made it back himself. The tourists, now genuinely unnerved, listen intently. Henry's face tightens — he's heard this kind of story too many times before.

Tom's fear is raw, palpable. He pleads with Henry to tell them more, to give them answers. But Henry looks around the room, taking in the skeptical, frightened faces. He decides it's enough for the night and abruptly ends the tour, ushering the tourists out into the storm.

Part 6: Confronting Fears

After the tour ends, the main characters linger, drawn together by the shared tension of what they've just heard. Claire begins to ask Henry pointed questions about the story, wanting to dig

deeper, but he's tight-lipped. She senses he's hiding something. Eddie, driven by his desire to find out what happened to his father, tries to pry more details from Henry about the truck driver's disappearance. Rachel nervously suggests they all go to Black Mountain together, thinking they might find some answers — or at least closure.

Derek, sensing a good opportunity for his YouTube channel, volunteers to film the adventure. He thinks it will make for great content and could help him confront his fear of the dark. The others are hesitant, but they're also intrigued — a part of them needs to see it for themselves.

They decide to meet the next evening at the base of Black Mountain, each driven by their own reasons

— fear, curiosity, grief, or a need for closure. As they leave the museum, a sense of unease settles over them. The storm outside has intensified, and the fog seems to be creeping down from the mountain, as if reaching out to them.

Henry watches them go, a deep worry in his eyes. He knows they're walking into something far more dangerous than they realize. He whispers under his breath, "Some things are better left alone," as he locks the museum door, a faint chill running down his spine.

CHAPTER 2: THE NEWCOMERS

Part 1: The Arrival of Outsiders

The chapter begins with a view of the winding road leading into Harlan, Kentucky. The weather is gloomy, with low-hanging fog and intermittent rain. The narrow road snakes through dense woods, the canopy overhead forming a dark tunnel. A car speeds along the road, carrying a group of four college students — **Sarah**, **Jake**, **Emily**, and **Chris** — who have come to Harlan for a weekend trip.

The group is lively, bantering back and forth, excited about their adventure. They've heard the tales of Headless Annie from a podcast on local legends, and they're eager to experience the thrill of visiting Black Mountain, despite the warnings they received from locals at a gas station earlier that day. Their conversation is peppered with both excitement and skepticism, with each of them revealing their initial attitudes toward the legend.

- **Sarah**, a psychology major, is analytical and determined to explore the psychological aspects of fear. She dismisses the story as a simple case of mass hysteria but is fascinated by why so many people believe in it. Her fear is deeply personal; she has a phobia of losing control after a traumatic experience with her father's erratic behavior during his final years, which ended in tragedy.

- **Jake** is the daredevil of the group, always looking for the next adrenaline rush. He jokes about challenging Annie, confident that she's nothing more than a story to scare kids. Underneath his bravado, he is afraid of being seen as weak or afraid. He has always been driven by his older brother's achievements, and he fears that his courage is the only thing that sets him apart.
- **Emily** is quiet and contemplative, a history major with a deep love for folklore. She grew up in a small town with its own ghost stories and has always felt a connection to the paranormal. She's terrified of the dark and has been since childhood when she experienced what she believed was a ghost encounter. She never talks about it, but the experience still haunts her.
- **Chris**, a journalism major, is intrigued by the potential of uncovering a big story. He has always been skeptical of anything he can't prove, but he secretly fears the unknown. He's afraid of the dark, of the things he cannot see or understand, stemming from a near-drowning incident when he was a child, trapped underwater in murky darkness.

As they drive, the fog thickens, and the road becomes more treacherous. They laugh nervously, but there is a palpable tension in the air. Chris checks his phone for directions, but the GPS signal cuts out, leaving them to navigate the mountain road blindly.

Part 2: Into the Fog

The car begins to sputter, and Jake curses under his breath as the engine stalls. The fog around them is so thick it feels almost solid, and the world outside the car becomes a shapeless gray. The group exchanges uneasy glances, and a cold, creeping fear starts to settle in.

Jake tries to restart the car, but it won't budge. Sarah tries to joke to lighten the mood, but her voice wavers. Emily peers out of the window, her breath fogging the glass, feeling as though something is watching them from the darkness.

She sees a faint, white shape moving in the mist but convinces herself it's a trick of the light.

Chris suggests they wait for a few minutes and try again, but the air feels thick with tension. Sarah, thinking about her father's paranoia and her own fear of losing control, suggests they all take a deep breath and relax, trying to keep everyone calm.

Her mind races with psychological explanations for the fear they're all feeling.

Suddenly, there's a loud knock on the window. They jump, and Emily lets out a scream. Jake,

embarrassed by his own reaction, gets out of the car to investigate, still putting on a show of bravado. He takes a flashlight and moves cautiously around the vehicle, his heartbeat echoing in his ears. The fog seems to close in around him, and he can't see more than a few feet in any direction.

Part 3: First Signs of Terror

Jake's flashlight catches a glimpse of something white moving through the fog. He freezes, suddenly unsure of himself. He calls out, "Hello? Who's there?" There is no answer, just the eerie stillness and the sound of his own breathing. He takes a few steps closer, and the shape becomes clearer — a figure in white, a woman standing still in the fog, her back to him.

He hesitates, feeling a cold chill down his spine. He calls out again, more forcefully this time. The figure doesn't move. He feels a sudden wave of dread but pushes it down, determined not to show fear. He steps closer, but then the figure starts to turn, slowly, agonizingly slowly.

Inside the car, Emily is staring out, her eyes wide. She sees the woman in white and grabs Sarah's arm. "Jake, get back in the car!" she screams, her voice breaking with fear. Jake doesn't move. He's transfixed, unable to look away as the figure turns to face him. And then he sees it — no head, just a gaping neck, with something dark and wet

glistening in the moonlight.

The figure begins to move toward him, and the fog thickens around them, swallowing them both.

Jake's bravado crumbles, and he turns to run, but he trips and falls, the flashlight spinning away into the darkness. He scrambles to his feet, heart pounding, and runs back toward the car.

As he reaches the car, he jumps in, slamming the door behind him. His face is pale, and he's breathing heavily. "Go! Go!" he shouts, but the car won't start. Chris is frantically turning the key, panic setting in. The fog outside seems to press against the windows, and they hear a faint humming sound, almost like a lullaby, echoing through the mist.

Part 4: Flashbacks and Revelations

While they wait in terror, each character experiences a flashback that reveals more about their fears and strengths.

- **Sarah**: She remembers being a little girl, hiding in her room while her father had one of his episodes. He was ranting and raving, convinced that someone was out to get him. She had been terrified of his unpredictability, of the way he could change in an instant. She's always feared losing control, either of herself or of a situation, and that fear is rising now as she

  sits in the car, powerless.

- **Jake**: He remembers a time when he was younger, and his older brother had dared him to climb a tall tree. He had been scared but didn't want to show it. He climbed, slipped, and fell, breaking his arm. His brother had laughed it off, but Jake had felt humiliated, weak. He's always pushed himself to prove he's not afraid, but deep down, he fears he's never been brave at all.

- **Emily**: She recalls a night when she was eight years old, lying in bed in her childhood home. She saw a shadowy figure standing at the foot of her bed. She had felt paralyzed, unable to scream or move, convinced it was a ghost. Her parents had told her it was just a nightmare, but she knew it was real. She's always been afraid of the dark, of what might be lurking just out of sight.
- **Chris**: He thinks back to the day he nearly drowned, the way the water had closed over his head, the darkness swallowing him up. He had been terrified, unable to see, unable to breathe, convinced he was going to die. He has never forgotten the feeling of helplessness, of being trapped in the dark, and he feels it again now, in the car, surrounded by fog.

The tension builds as each character confronts their fears in the silence of the car. The humming outside grows louder, and they feel a cold chill creeping through the windows. Sarah tries to steady her breathing, whispering that it's just their minds playing tricks on them. Jake, shaken, refuses to look back at the figure in the fog, now much closer, its headless body barely visible.

Suddenly, there's a loud bang on the roof of the car, and the entire group jumps. Chris shouts for everyone to stay quiet and locks all the doors. The sound grows louder, like something scraping across the metal, and they feel the car shift slightly, as if something heavy is moving on top of it.

Part 5: The First Encounter

The group is on the edge of panic. Jake, who had always prided himself on his courage, is visibly shaken, his hands trembling. Emily is muttering a prayer under her breath, her eyes darting around the car. Chris tries the ignition again, and this time, the car roars to life. Relief washes over them, but it's short-lived. The car lurches forward, but they realize the headlights are dimming, flickering.

They can barely see the road ahead, and the fog seems to be moving, swirling around them as if alive. The humming is now almost deafening, and Sarah feels a sudden wave of nausea. She grips the seat, trying to hold on to some semblance of control.

As they drive, they see a shadow move quickly

across the road in front of them. Chris slams on the brakes, but the car skids, sliding sideways. They hear a blood-curdling scream, and for a moment, they

CHAPTER 3: THE DESCENT INTO DARKNESS

Part 1: Preparations for the Night

The next day, the weather in Lynch, Kentucky, is grim and oppressive. The storm has passed, but a thick fog still clings to the town, seeping into every corner like a creeping phantom. The sky is a dull, heavy gray, and a chilling wind sweeps through the streets. The group of locals — Claire, Eddie, Rachel, and Derek — meet at a local diner to prepare for their planned trip up Black Mountain that evening.

The tension between them is palpable as they gather around a corner booth. They're all uneasy, aware that they're venturing into dangerous territory, but each of them has their reasons for going.

- **Claire Morgan** is focused and intent on gathering information for her article. She's brought a notebook filled with questions and research notes about Black Mountain and the legend of Headless Annie. Her skepticism drives her to get to the bottom of the story, but she is battling her fear of the unknown. Her motivation is deeply rooted in the loss of her father, whose

mysterious disappearance left her desperate for answers. She's determined not to be haunted by another unresolved mystery.

- **Eddie Lee** sits quietly, sipping coffee, his weathered face betraying a mix of determination and apprehension. He's brought an old map of Black Mountain, one his father had used when he was a truck driver. The map is covered in faded notes, including one that marks the spot where his father disappeared. Eddie's fear of the mountain is coupled with the trauma of losing his father, but he's resolved to face it head-on. His strength lies in his resilience and his desire to confront his past.

- **Rachel Thompson** is visibly nervous. She's fidgeting with a charm bracelet her grandmother gave her for protection against evil spirits. Her faith in the supernatural is unshakeable, but she's also plagued by a deep fear of the mountain and the malevolent spirit that supposedly haunts it. However, Rachel has an unspoken inner strength: a deep empathy and a connection to the paranormal that she has experienced since she was a child.
- **Derek Sullivan** is excited, his camera equipment spread across the table. He sees this as a perfect opportunity for his YouTube channel, and he talks about it as if it's just another adventure. But his bravado

is a thin veneer covering his real fear — a fear of the dark that he's never quite managed to shake off. Derek's strength lies in his optimism and adaptability, his ability to think on his feet, but his fear is very real.

They discuss their plan for the evening. Claire suggests they split up to cover more ground, but Eddie disagrees, insisting that they should stick together for safety. Rachel, clutching her charm bracelet, agrees with Eddie, believing that the spirit is more likely to attack when they're separated. Derek is eager to go off on his own, thinking it will make for better footage. The tension mounts as they argue, but they eventually agree to stay together.

Henry Calloway, the museum curator, arrives unexpectedly and pulls Claire aside. He warns her again about the dangers of going up the mountain at night. His face is lined with worry, and his voice trembles as he tells her about the last group that went up there — and how only one came back, incoherent and broken. He gives her an old, weathered book filled with newspaper clippings and handwritten notes about Headless Annie, hoping it might help them understand what they're up against.

Part 2: The Ascent Begins

As evening approaches, the group drives to the base of Black Mountain. The fog has thickened,

and the temperature drops sharply. The woods are silent, almost unnaturally so. Even the birds seem to have gone quiet, and the only sound is the crunch of gravel under their boots as they step out of the car.

They're armed with flashlights, a portable radio, and Derek's camera equipment. Claire takes the lead, trying to project confidence, but her hands tremble slightly as she flips through Henry's book, looking for any clue that might guide them. Eddie holds the map, his eyes fixed on the spot marked with his father's disappearance, while Rachel murmurs a prayer under her breath, holding onto her charm bracelet. Derek is already filming, talking excitedly to the camera, try-ing to capture the eerie atmosphere.

The path up the mountain is narrow and overgrown, the fog wrapping around them like a living thing. Every step feels heavier, the silence pressing down on them. Eddie, feeling a sense of foreboding, stops to check the map again. He tells the others that the path they're on is one of the last routes his father took before disappearing. Claire insists they keep moving, feeling an urgent need to reach the heart of the mountain.

Rachel starts to feel a strange tingling sensation, as if someone is watching them. She turns to Derek and whispers that they're not alone, but he brushes it off, saying it's just nerves. Rachel clutches her bracelet tighter, her fear growing with every step.

Suddenly, they hear a soft, distant humming — the same eerie lullaby that the college students had heard the night before. The sound sends a chill through the group, freezing them in place. Derek turns the camera toward the sound, his face betraying a mix of excitement and fear.

Part 3: The First Signs

As they continue up the path, the fog seems to grow denser, and the humming becomes louder. They come across an old, abandoned truck, its headlights shattered, covered in rust and ivy.

Eddie's breath catches in his throat as he recognizes it — it's the truck his father drove before he disappeared. He rushes over, desperate to find some clue, some sign of what happened.

Inside, they find a notebook, the pages yellowed and brittle. Eddie opens it and begins to read aloud, his voice trembling. The notebook is filled with his father's writing — notes about strange sounds, glimpses of a figure in white, and the feeling of being followed. Eddie's hands shake as he reads the final entry, dated the day his father vanished: "She's here. I can feel her. I don't think I'm getting off this mountain alive."

Eddie's face crumples, a mixture of grief and fear. Claire puts a hand on his shoulder, offering silent support. Rachel steps forward, feeling a strange energy emanating from the truck. She closes her eyes and begins to whisper a protective prayer, sensing the presence of something malevolent.

Derek, sensing a great moment for his channel, films everything, his excitement mounting. But he's also starting to feel the weight of the darkness around them. He hears a rustling in the bushes and points his camera toward it, but sees nothing. His heart races, and he tightens his grip on the camera, trying to steady his nerves.

The humming stops abruptly, and the silence is deafening. They all freeze, waiting, listening. Then, a branch snaps in the distance, followed by a faint whisper that seems to echo through the fog.

It's a woman's voice, soft and mournful, calling a name they can't quite make out.

Part 4: Encounters with the Unknown

The group decides to press on, but the atmosphere is tense, the air thick with fear. Claire leads the way, her flashlight cutting a narrow path through the fog. She tries to focus on her notes, looking for any clues that might help them, but her mind keeps drifting back to her father's disappearance. She's determined to face whatever is up there, to prove to herself that she's not afraid.

As they move deeper into the woods, the path becomes more difficult to navigate. The trees seem to close in around them, their gnarled branches reaching out like skeletal hands. The fog is thicker here, almost suffocating, and they have to stay close together to avoid getting lost.

Suddenly, Rachel gasps and points to a figure standing in the distance. It's a woman in white, her back turned to them. The figure seems to shimmer in the fog, almost ethereal. Derek raises his camera, trying to get a clear shot, but the figure fades, disappearing into the mist.

Eddie, his heart pounding, shouts after her, calling her name — "Annie!" — but there's no response. Claire urges him to stay quiet, fearing they might provoke whatever is out there. Rachel begins to feel a sharp pain in her chest, as if something is squeezing her heart. She clutches her charm bracelet, praying harder, tears streaming down her face.

Derek's camera suddenly flickers, and he curses under his breath, tapping the screen. When it comes back on, he freezes. On the screen, he sees a face — pale, with dark, hollow eyes, staring directly at him. He spins around, but there's nothing there. He tries to laugh it off, but his voice shakes.

Then, the humming returns, louder this time, and closer. It seems to be coming from all directions, echoing through the trees. The group huddles together, their flashlights darting around, searching for the source of the sound. The fog swirls around them, and they hear a soft whisper, a name repeated over and over: "Martha... Martha..."

Henry had mentioned the name before — his sister, who had disappeared decades ago. Claire's heart races as she realizes that whatever is out

there knows more about them than they could have imagined. She feels a chill run down her spine, a cold sweat breaking out on her forehead.

Part 5: Confronting Their Fears

The whispering grows louder, and the group becomes more frantic. The sound is haunting, reverberating through the fog like a chant. **Claire** realizes that the spirit — or whatever it is — seems to be calling out to each of them, knowing their names, their secrets, their fears. Her mind races as she tries to find a rational explanation, but deep down, she feels the grip of panic tightening around her. Her father's face flashes in her mind, and for a moment, she thinks she hears his voice among the whispers, calling her name. It shakes her to her core.

Eddie is on edge, gripping his flashlight so tightly that his knuckles are white. He feels like he's back in his childhood home, hiding from the shadows that his father would talk about. The voice calling "Martha" reminds him of how his father used to talk to someone who wasn't there, a ghost from his past. Eddie knows that if he turns and runs now, he'll never find out what happened to his father, but every instinct tells him to flee. His hands tremble, but he takes a deep breath, steeling himself. He's not a scared little boy anymore — he won't run this time.

Rachel senses the energy around them changing, becoming more malevolent. She feels an intense pressure on her chest, like an invisible hand squeezing her heart. Her breaths become shallow, and she closes her eyes, whispering a prayer louder, desperately seeking protection. Her grandmother's voice echoes in her mind, "Faith is your shield." She repeats the words like a mantra, clinging to her faith as her only protection. The whispering grows louder, and she feels something cold brush against her arm. She flinches, opening her eyes, but sees nothing. She knows they're being tested — their fears exploited.

Derek is no longer filming; his camera hangs loosely by his side. The thrill he felt earlier is gone, replaced by a deep, gnawing dread. He tries to make light of the situation, cracking a joke, but his voice sounds hollow and strained. He remembers a night from his childhood, trapped in the basement during a power outage, the darkness swallowing him whole. He had screamed for hours until his parents found him. The memory of that darkness feels all too real now, closing in around him. His hands are shaking, but he forces himself to keep the camera rolling, as if the lens is a barrier between him and whatever is out there.

The whispers suddenly stop, replaced by an eerie silence. The fog parts slightly, revealing a small, dilapidated cabin up ahead, its windows dark and broken. The group hesitates. Claire suggests that they go inside, thinking there might be clues or something to help them understand what's happening. Eddie is reluctant, but he knows they need to keep moving. Rachel, feeling a strong pull toward the cabin, nods in agreement. Derek hesitates, torn between his fear and the potential for a great story.

They approach the cabin slowly, flashlights sweeping over the rotting wood and broken windows. The door creaks open on its own, a low, mournful sound that sends a chill through them.

They step inside, and the air is immediately colder, almost freezing. The cabin smells of mold and decay, the walls covered in faded, yellowing newspapers. There's an old rocking chair in the corner, moving slowly as if recently touched.

Part 6: The Haunted Cabin

Inside the cabin, the group feels an overwhelming sense of dread. The air is thick, almost suffocating. Claire examines the newspapers on the walls, realizing they are all clippings about missing people from the town — names and faces that seem eerily familiar. One of the clippings catches her eye: a picture of a woman with dark hair and a kind smile, labeled "Martha Calloway — Missing, 1953." Claire's hand shakes as she realizes this is Henry Calloway's sister, the name they had heard in the whispers.

Eddie, still holding his father's notebook, sees a drawing on the wall — a crude sketch of the truck they found earlier, and next to it, a figure in white, headless. His father's handwriting is scrawled beneath it: "She watches... always watching." His heart races as he feels the weight of his father's fear, the terror that had haunted him until his disappearance.

Rachel moves toward a small wooden table in the center of the room, where an old, dusty Bible sits. She opens it cautiously, and a faded photograph falls out. It's a picture of a young girl, no more than eight, standing in front of the same cabin. Her eyes are wide, and she looks terrified. On the back of the photo, someone has written, "Forgive me." Rachel feels a wave of sadness wash over her, sensing a tragic story hidden in these walls.

Derek, trying to distract himself from his fear, starts filming again, focusing on the eerie details of the cabin. As he pans the camera around, he catches a glimpse of movement in the viewfinder. He lowers the camera and turns to see a shadow darting past one of the windows. "Did you see that?" he whispers, his voice barely audible. The others turn, and Claire shines her flashlight toward the window, but there's nothing there.

Suddenly, they hear the sound of footsteps on the porch, slow and deliberate. The door creaks open wider, and a cold wind rushes in, extinguishing their flashlights for a moment. When they flicker back on, they see a figure standing in the doorway

— a woman in a white dress, headless, her hands stretched out toward them.

Panic sets in. Claire shouts for everyone to move, but they are frozen with fear. The figure steps closer, and they feel an overwhelming sense of dread. Eddie drops the notebook and grabs a chair, ready to defend himself, but the woman stops, her headless form swaying slightly, as if listening to something.

Rachel, trembling, steps forward, holding out her charm bracelet. She begins to pray loudly, her voice steadying with each word. The figure seems to hesitate, as if it's struggling against an unseen force. Derek, sensing an opportunity, begins to film, but his hands are shaking too much to keep the camera steady.

Claire takes a deep breath, forcing herself to think. She remembers a line from Henry's book — something about Headless Annie being bound to the mountain by an old curse, a curse tied to a betrayal. "She's trapped here," Claire mutters, piecing together the clues. "We need to find out what binds her. Maybe we can set her free."

The figure suddenly vanishes, leaving only the sound of the wind and their own ragged breathing. They exchange nervous glances, realizing they've only just begun to unravel the mystery.

Part 7: Breaking the Curse

Determined to end the nightmare, Claire leads the group in searching the cabin for more clues.

Rachel continues to pray, sensing a faint, benevolent energy in the room now, as if someone

— or something — is guiding them. Eddie picks up the Bible and flips through the pages, finding a handwritten note tucked between them. The note is old and faded, but the words are still legible: "To break the bond, find the one who betrayed. Only then can the spirit be freed."

Derek looks around, confused. "Who betrayed her?" he asks, his voice tense. Claire thinks back to the newspaper clippings, remembering Henry's warning about Martha. "Maybe it wasn't Headless Annie who was betrayed," she says slowly. "Maybe it was Martha — and that's why the spirit won't rest."

They decide to head deeper into the mountain, following the path that Eddie's father had marked on the map. The fog thickens again, and they hear the faint sound of crying, a woman's voice carried on the wind. Rachel feels a pull, an inexplicable urge to follow the sound. "She's leading us," she whispers, convinced that Martha's spirit is trying to communicate with them.

As they trek further, the path becomes narrower and more treacherous. They hear rustling in the bushes and see fleeting shadows moving just beyond their vision. Derek keeps the camera rolling, his fear mounting, but he's determined to capture everything. Eddie clutches the notebook, scanning the trees for any sign of the figure they saw earlier.

They come to a clearing and find an old, crumbling headstone, half-buried under leaves and dirt. The name "Martha Calloway" is etched into the stone, but it looks like it was scratched out violently, as if someone didn't want it to be remembered. Beside it, a second, smaller headstone reads, "Annie — Beloved Daughter."

Claire kneels by the headstones, brushing away the dirt. She realizes that Martha was Annie's mother, and that she had been searching for her lost child when she disappeared. The betrayal wasn't just against Annie; it was against Martha, who had been falsely accused of a crime she didn't commit. Claire feels a surge of determination. "We need to clear her name," she says, standing up. "That's the only way to break the curse."

Eddie, determined to help, starts digging around the headstones with his bare hands, looking for any more clues. Derek films, capturing every moment, while Rachel continues her prayers, sensing that they are close to the truth.

Part 8: The Final Confrontation

As Eddie digs, he uncovers a small, rusted box buried beneath the earth. He pries it open, revealing a collection

Part 8: The Final Confrontation

As Eddie pries open the rusted box, its contents spill out: a collection of old letters, a lock of dark hair, a silver locket, and a small, weathered diary.

The diary is wrapped in a delicate piece of white cloth, stained and frayed from years in the ground. Eddie carefully picks it up and hands it to Claire, who opens it with trembling hands. Inside, they find entries written in a hurried, shaky hand — Martha's.

The entries tell a heart-wrenching story: Martha Calloway was falsely accused of murdering her daughter, Annie, after a horrific accident on the mountain. Martha's pleas of innocence went unheard, and the townspeople, convinced by fear and superstition, blamed her for Annie's death. In her grief, Martha searched the mountain for Annie's spirit, believing that her daughter was still wandering, lost and alone. But instead, she disappeared too, her name tarnished and her soul unable to rest.

Rachel, with her connection to the spiritual, senses the deep anguish emanating from the diary. She softly reads one of the last entries aloud: "I have searched these woods every night. I hear her crying for me, but I cannot find her. I am so afraid. Forgive me, Annie. Forgive me..."

As she finishes reading, the wind around them picks up, howling through the trees with a mournful wail. The temperature drops sharply, and the fog thickens again, swirling around them like grasping hands. Claire quickly flips through the remaining pages, hoping to find something that will help. One entry catches her eye, the writing more frantic: "If you ever find this, know that I loved my daughter. I did not harm her. Find the

locket — find the truth..."

Claire looks down at the silver locket that had spilled from the box. She picks it up and carefully opens it, revealing a faded photograph of a young girl — Annie — and a lock of her hair. On the back of the locket, engraved in small, elegant script, are the words, "For my beloved Annie, forever in my heart."

Suddenly, they hear a rustling behind them. The group turns, hearts pounding, to see the figure of Headless Annie materializing in the fog, standing just beyond the edge of the clearing. Her headless form sways slowly, and her hands are outstretched toward them. But this time, the figure does not advance; instead, it seems to be waiting, almost hesitant.

Claire takes a deep breath and steps forward, holding the locket out in front of her. "Annie," she calls out, her voice wavering but firm. "Your mother loved you. She didn't hurt you. She was looking for you, just like you've been looking for her."

The figure pauses, as if listening. Rachel, sensing they're getting through, steps forward and joins Claire. "Annie," she says softly, "we're here to help you both find peace. We know the truth now. You don't have to be alone anymore."

The wind howls louder, and the fog swirls violently around them, but the figure of Headless Annie remains still, seeming almost to soften.

Then, from the shadows behind her, another figure emerges — that of a woman in a torn white dress, her face streaked with dirt and tears. Martha Calloway's spirit, the mother who never stopped searching for her lost child.

Martha's spirit reaches out toward Annie, her hands trembling, her eyes filled with sorrow and love. "Annie... my sweet Annie..." she whispers, her voice carried on the wind. The headless figure slowly turns, as if recognizing the voice, and begins to walk toward Martha.

Eddie, Derek, Rachel, and Claire hold their breath, watching as the two spirits move closer together. The air is thick with tension, and the fog swirls around them, growing more intense. For a moment, it feels as if the entire world has stopped, waiting.

Finally, the two figures meet. Martha reaches out, gently touching the place where Annie's head should be. "I'm sorry, Annie," she whispers, tears streaming down her ghostly face. "I'm so sorry…"

There is a moment of stillness, and then, in an instant, the fog dissipates, lifting like a veil being pulled away. The air becomes warmer, and the oppressive weight that had hung over them vanishes. The headless figure of Annie shimmers, and a soft light begins to emanate from within her. Slowly, her form becomes whole — her head reappears, her face soft and peaceful. She looks at her mother with a look of understanding and love.

The two spirits embrace, and a calm, serene smile spreads across Annie's face. The group watches in

awe as the spirits begin to fade, their forms growing more transparent with each passing moment. As they disappear, they hear a faint, whispered "Thank you…" carried on the wind.

Part 9: Aftermath and Reflection

The group stands in the clearing, the silence almost deafening after the intensity of the encounter. The fog has completely lifted, and the stars are visible above them, twinkling in the night sky. The oppressive chill has gone, replaced by a gentle, soothing breeze.

Eddie falls to his knees, overwhelmed by emotion. For the first time in years, he feels a sense of peace regarding his father's disappearance. He knows now that his father's death was not in vain; his father had been trying to bring an end to this haunting, just as they did tonight. Eddie picks up the old notebook and tucks it into his jacket, a silent promise to carry on his father's memory with honor.

Derek, still filming, finally lowers his camera. He realizes the footage he captured is more than he could have hoped for, but he also feels changed by what he witnessed. The fear that gripped him has given way to a deeper understanding of the unknown. He knows this story is more than just content for his channel — it's a tribute to the restless spirits who found peace tonight.

Rachel breathes deeply, feeling a warm glow inside her, a sense of relief and fulfillment. Her faith had been tested, but she remained strong, and now she feels closer to her spiritual beliefs than ever. She knows she will never forget the faces of Martha and Annie, nor the profound connection she felt with them.

Claire stands quietly, holding the locket in her hand. She feels a profound sense of closure, not only for Annie and Martha but for herself. The mystery of the mountain has been solved, and in the process, she has faced her own fears and doubts. She decides that she will write this story, not as a horror tale, but as a testament to love, loss, and the unbreakable bond between a mother and her child.

As they turn to leave, they hear the sound of gentle laughter — a child's laughter, soft and pure, echoing through the woods. They smile, knowing that Annie and Martha have finally found peace.

The group begins the descent down Black Mountain, the weight lifted from their shoulders. The darkness no longer seems threatening but instead feels like a quiet, welcoming blanket. They know they will never forget what happened here, but they also know they have done something important, something meaningful.

As they reach the bottom of the mountain, the first light of dawn begins to break over the horizon, casting a golden glow over the town of Lynch.

They walk back to their cars in silence, each lost in

their thoughts, but they all feel the same — a sense of calm, a sense of resolution, and a sense that, for the first time in a long time, they are no longer afraid.

With the spirits of Black Mountain at rest, the town of Lynch can finally breathe again. And as Claire, Eddie, Rachel, and Derek return to their lives, they carry with them a story that will be told for generations — a story of love, loss, and the power of truth to set even the most restless spirits free.

CHAPTER 4: INTO THE FOG

Section 1: Entering the Unknown

The group gathers at the base of Black Mountain, the air thick with anticipation and a creeping fog that has begun to roll down the slope like an encroaching tide. Claire, Eddie, Rachel, and Derek stand in a tense circle around their cars, their breath visible in the chilling air. Each of them is armed with flashlights, walkie-talkies, and backpacks filled with supplies — not that any of it seems like enough.

Claire is trying to steady her nerves, reviewing the map one last time. She's aware that she's the de facto leader, whether she wants the role or not. Her academic training tells her to stay rational, but the unsettling feeling in her gut is harder to shake. She

remembers the stories her grandmother used to tell her about spirits who never found peace, and she wonders if Annie is one of them. Her mind races back to the day she saw her grandmother's face, etched with fear, warning her never to come near this mountain. But here she is, driven by a need to find answers — not just for the missing people but also for the haunting mystery of her own past.

Eddie is going through his father's old notes, re- reading every line, every sketch, as if seeking some final piece of guidance from beyond the grave. He's trying to connect the dots between what his father wrote and what they're about to face. His father had written about the fog — "It's alive, it moves with purpose," the words say, and Eddie can't help but think of the old man, eyes wide, speaking of the fog like a living creature. Eddie's determination is driven by a promise he made to himself when his father vanished: he would not stop until he found out what truly happened. Yet fear claws at him — the fear of facing the same fate, of disappearing into the unknown without a trace, just like his father.

Rachel is silent, clutching her charm bracelet, her lips moving in prayer. Her faith is her shield, but tonight it feels tested like never before. She's thinking of her brother, David, lost to addiction, wandering into the fog of his own despair and never coming back. She had always believed she could save him, if only she could find the right way, say the right words. Now, on this fog-covered mountain, she feels the same desperate urge — to

save those who are lost, to protect the living from the dead. But what if her faith isn't strong enough? What if her prayers fall on deaf ears? She shudders, tightening her grip on the charm bracelet, feeling the familiar weight of her grandmother's old cross against her chest.

Derek is jittery, holding his camera up to his eye, capturing everything. This is the kind of footage that could make him a star, the kind of story people would remember. But there's a deep-seated fear gnawing at him. He remembers being a child, scared of the dark, hiding under his covers while his mother screamed in the next room. He remembers the nights spent in the closet, clutching his ears, trying to block out the sounds of his parents' violent arguments. The dark had always been a place where secrets were kept, where bad things happened. And now, as he films the dense fog curling around them, he wonders if he is just running back into the darkness, hoping this time it will be different. Hoping he will survive.

As they step onto the trail leading up the mountain, the fog seems to thicken, becoming almost tangible. It's as if it has a life of its own, swirling around their ankles, pulling them in deeper. Claire holds the map tightly, trying to stay focused, while Eddie looks around with a wary eye. Rachel mutters prayers under her breath, and Derek keeps his camera rolling, documenting every step, every breath.

Section 2: The First Encounter

The path narrows as they ascend, the fog growing denser with each step. The sound of their footsteps is muffled, and they can barely see a few feet in front of them. Suddenly, a low, guttural sound echoes from the woods to their left. They freeze, exchanging nervous glances.

"What was that?" Derek whispers, his camera aimed toward the trees.

"An animal," Claire replies, though she doesn't sound convinced. She tries to push down the rising panic in her chest.

But Eddie is staring hard into the fog, his face pale. "That didn't sound like an animal," he says. "It sounded like... like someone breathing."

Rachel clutches her charm bracelet tighter, her prayers growing louder. "God, protect us," she mutters, her voice trembling.

Suddenly, the fog shifts, revealing a figure standing in the middle of the path ahead — a man, tall and thin, with a face hidden in shadow. Claire's breath catches in her throat. The man is standing unnaturally still, his head slightly tilted as if listening for something. She steps forward, trying to see more clearly, but before she can say anything, the figure dissolves into the fog.

"What the hell was that?" Derek gasps, lowering his camera for a moment.

Claire shakes her head. "I... I don't know. Did anyone else see that?"

Eddie nods, his face tight with fear. "Yeah. I saw it. We need to keep moving. Standing still isn't safe."

They continue up the path, but the mood has shifted. The air feels heavier, more oppressive. Claire checks the map again, noticing that they're approaching a bend in the trail where several disappearances were reported in Henry's journal. Her heart pounds in her chest as they approach the bend, the fog so thick now that it feels like they're walking through a cloud.

Suddenly, a cold wind sweeps through the trees, and they hear the sound of whispering — soft, indistinguishable voices carried on the wind.

Rachel stops, her face pale. "Do you hear that?" she whispers.

Claire nods, her grip on the map tightening. "It's coming from up ahead," she says. "We need to be careful."

They inch forward, every step feeling heavier than the last. As they round the bend, they see it — an old, rusted truck, abandoned on the side of the path, its windows shattered and its doors wide open. Eddie's heart sinks. It's the same truck from his father's sketch.

"That's... that's my dad's truck," he whispers, his voice breaking. He rushes forward, ignoring Claire's warning to be careful. He reaches the truck and peers inside, his breath fogging up in the cold air. The interior is coated in a thick layer of dust, and on the passenger seat, he finds a single, bloodstained glove.

Eddie feels his heart hammering in his chest. He remembers his father's notes, the descriptions of the fog, the fear in his voice when he spoke of the mountain. "It's like he just... disappeared," Eddie mutters, his eyes scanning the truck for any more clues.

But then the whispering grows louder, and the fog swirls around them with renewed intensity. Claire grabs Eddie's arm, pulling him back from the truck. "We need to keep moving," she urges. "This place... it's not safe."

Suddenly, a cold hand brushes against Claire's cheek. She gasps and whirls around, but there's no one there. Derek catches the moment on camera, his hands trembling. "Did you feel that?" he asks, his voice barely audible.

Claire nods, her skin prickling with fear. "Something... touched me," she whispers.

Rachel steps forward, holding up her charm bracelet. "We're not alone," she says softly. "Something is watching us."

The fog shifts again, and they hear a soft, childlike giggle echoing through the trees. Claire feels her stomach drop. "Annie," she whispers. "She's here."

Section 3: Descent into Madness

As they press on, the fog thickens even further, wrapping around them like a cold, damp shroud.

The whispering voices grow louder, and they hear footsteps crunching on the leaves behind them.

Eddie turns, shining his flashlight into the fog, but there's nothing there. Just shadows and mist.

Derek begins to sweat, his camera shaking in his hands. "I don't like this, man," he mutters. "I don't like this at all."

"Stay close," Claire orders, her voice tense. "Don't wander off."

But the voices grow louder, more insistent. They hear names being called out, names that send chills down their spines — **Rachel's brother, Eddie's father, Claire's grandmother, Derek's mother**.

Each name is spoken in a different voice, some familiar, some foreign, but all dripping with malice.

Rachel begins to panic. "They know us," she whispers, her voice trembling. "They know who we are…"

The fog begins to swirl around them faster, and suddenly, they see the figure of a woman in a white dress, standing on the path ahead, headless and motionless. Claire stops dead in her tracks, her heart pounding in her ears. "Annie," she breathes, her voice barely a whisper.

The figure doesn't move, but the air around them seems to grow colder, the fog thickening into a solid wall of white. Claire feels a surge of fear and determination. She knows they need to confront this spirit, to find out what it wants.

"Annie," Claire calls out, her voice stronger. "We know about you. We know you were

Section 4: A Haunting Revelation

Claire's voice cuts through the thick fog like a knife. "Annie, we know you were lost, that you were searching for your mother. We're here to help you. Tell us what you need."

The headless figure remains still for a moment, then slowly begins to move. It doesn't walk but seems to glide over the ground, drifting toward them with an eerie, unnatural grace. The temperature drops sharply, their breaths coming out in frosty puffs. Claire stands her ground, though every instinct in her body screams to run. Behind her, Rachel grips her charm bracelet tighter, murmuring prayers under her breath, her eyes wide with terror.

Eddie's face is pale, but there's a fire in his eyes. "We're here to find the truth," he says, taking a step forward. "We're not leaving until we know what happened to you, and to everyone else."

As if in response, the fog swirls faster around them, whipping at their faces like icy tendrils. The whispers return, louder and more distinct, filled with anger and despair. "Leave... leave... leave..." they chant, over and over, a chorus of tormented souls. The ground beneath them begins to tremble, small stones and leaves vibrating with the intensity.

Derek's camera flickers, the screen filled with

static. "This is... this is insane," he mutters, trying to steady his hands. "Are we sure we should be doing this?"

Before anyone can answer, the fog parts slightly, revealing a small, dilapidated cabin just off the path, its wooden door hanging off one hinge. The windows are shattered, and the roof looks ready to collapse. A faint, ghostly light flickers inside, like a candle burning in the dark.

"That wasn't there before," Rachel whispers, her eyes wide.

Claire nods, her heart pounding. "No, it wasn't. But I think we're meant to go inside."

Eddie swallows hard, his mind racing with memories of his father's tales of the mountain. "That cabin... my dad mentioned it in his notes," he says, his voice shaky. "He called it 'Annie's Rest.'"

The group approaches the cabin cautiously, the door creaking open as if inviting them in. Inside, the air is thick with the scent of damp wood and decay. The faint light seems to come from a small lantern on a dusty table in the corner, flickering like it could go out at any moment.

They step inside, one by one, their footsteps echoing on the wooden floor. The atmosphere is suffocating, heavy with an unseen presence. The walls are covered in faded, peeling wallpaper, and there are old, broken pieces of furniture scattered around. On the table, they see a collection of items

— an old, rusted doll, a yellowed photograph of a young girl, and a hand-stitched handkerchief with the initials "A.C." embroidered in the corner.

"That must be Annie's," Claire whispers, reaching out to touch the handkerchief. As her fingers make contact, the lantern suddenly flares brighter, casting long, ominous shadows on the walls. The temperature drops again, and the voices return, this time clearer and more desperate.

"Mama... Mama... help me..."

Rachel gasps, her heart clenching. "That's... that's a child's voice," she whispers, tears forming in her eyes.

Eddie feels a chill run down his spine. "Annie," he murmurs, "is that you?"

The voice changes, becoming softer, almost pleading. "Mama... where are you...?"

Claire, feeling a surge of empathy, steps forward. "We're here, Annie. We're here to help you find peace."

The air grows colder still, and they hear a low, rumbling growl from the shadows. The lantern flickers, and suddenly, the cabin feels smaller, the walls closing in around them. Derek's camera flickers again, and he sees something on the screen

— a shadowy figure standing just behind Claire, its eyes glowing a faint, eerie blue.

"Claire!" Derek shouts, reaching out to grab her. "Behind you!"

Claire spins around, but there's nothing there. "What did you see?" she demands, her voice tight with fear.

Derek's face is pale. "I... I don't know. It was like a shadow, but... it had eyes."

Rachel clutches her charm bracelet, her prayers becoming more frantic. "We need to leave," she whispers. "This place... it's not right."

Eddie shakes his head. "No. We can't leave. Not yet. We're close to something, I can feel it."

Suddenly, the whispers grow louder, a cacophony of voices rising in anguish. The floor beneath them trembles, and the walls begin to shake. The lantern flickers violently, and then, with a loud pop, it goes out, plunging them into darkness.

For a moment, there is nothing but silence and the sound of their ragged breathing. Then, from the corner of the room, a soft, ghostly light begins to glow, illuminating the figure of a young girl — Annie. She stands in a white dress, her head missing, but her posture is strangely calm, almost serene.

Eddie steps forward, his voice shaking. "Annie... we want to help you. Please, tell us what you need."

The figure of Annie tilts its head, as if listening. Then, in a voice that seems to come from everywhere and nowhere, they hear, "Find... the truth..."

Section 5: The Truth Unveiled

The room is filled with a sudden rush of wind, and the walls begin to change, shifting like a mirage. The peeling wallpaper fades away, revealing a different scene — a well-kept home, with a warm fire crackling in the hearth. They see a woman standing by the window, her face drawn and worried. It's Martha Calloway, Annie's mother.

The group watches in stunned silence as the scene unfolds like a film. Martha is speaking to someone, her voice filled with desperation. "She's gone... my little girl is gone," she sobs. "They took her... they took her away from me..."

A shadowy figure enters the room — a man, his face hidden in darkness. "You need to let it go, Martha," he says, his voice cold. "Annie's gone. There's nothing you can do."

Martha turns on him, her face twisted with grief. "No! I won't accept that! I know she's out there, I can feel it!"

The figure steps closer, his voice dripping with malice. "If you keep searching, you'll end up just like her... lost, alone, wandering these woods forever."

The room grows colder, and the scene begins to fade. The group finds themselves back in the dilapidated cabin, the air thick with tension.

"What... what was that?" Derek asks, his voice trembling.

Claire's mind races. "It was a memory," she says.

"A memory of what happened to Martha after Annie disappeared. Someone wanted her to stop searching... someone who knew more than they let on."

Eddie clenches his fists. "But why? Why did they want her to stop?"

Rachel steps forward, her eyes filled with determination. "Because they were hiding something. Something they didn't want her to find."

The whispers return, louder and more insistent, filling the room with a deafening roar. The walls tremble, and the floor begins to crack. Claire feels a surge of panic. "We need to get out of here," she shouts.

But before they can move, the ground beneath them gives way, and they fall into darkness, the world spinning around them...

Section 6: Descent into Darkness

They land hard on a cold, damp floor, their bodies aching from the impact. The air is thick with dust and the smell of earth. They are in a tunnel, the walls rough and uneven, lit only by the faint glow of phosphorescent moss.

Eddie groans, pushing himself up. "Is everyone okay?" he asks, his voice echoing off the stone walls.

Derek checks his camera, relieved to see it's still working. "Yeah, I think so," he mutters. "But

where the hell are we?"

Rachel looks around, her eyes wide with fear. "We're underground," she whispers. "But... how did we get here?"

Claire stands up, dusting herself off. "It doesn't matter," she says. "We need to keep moving.

There's something down here... something that will give us the answers we need."

They begin to walk, the tunnel stretching out before them like a dark, winding snake. The whispers follow them, growing louder and more insistent, urging them deeper into the darkness.

And as they move forward, they can't shake the feeling that they're not alone — that something is watching them from the shadows, waiting for the right moment to strike...

CHAPTER 5: THE SECRETS BENEATH THE MOUNTAIN

Section 1: Into the Abyss

The darkness of the tunnel seems to stretch on forever, swallowing every bit of light and hope. The group moves cautiously, their footsteps echoing against the damp stone walls. Each step

feels heavier than the last, weighed down by the oppressive atmosphere. The phosphorescent moss on the walls casts an eerie, greenish glow that barely illuminates their path, leaving more shadows than light.

Claire leads the way, her face set with determination, but inside, she's battling a storm of fear and uncertainty. She thinks about her childhood, how she'd always been the brave one, leading her friends on adventures through the woods. But this... this was different. This felt like walking into the jaws of some ancient beast. She pushes down her fear, focusing on the task ahead.

Behind her, Eddie's thoughts are racing. Memories of his father flood his mind — the late-night stories, the warnings about Black Mountain, the deep-seated fear in his father's eyes every time he mentioned Annie. Eddie had always brushed it off as superstition, but now, he felt the truth clawing at him. His father knew something, something terrible, and Eddie was terrified he'd end up just like him — a man haunted by what he could never fully understand.

Derek grips his camera tightly, using it like a lifeline. The digital screen flickers, distorting the shadows around them. His heartbeat pounds in his ears. He's been in dangerous places before, documenting natural disasters and war zones, but this... this was different. This wasn't a danger you could see or fight. This was something he couldn't rationalize or explain away, and it terrified him.

Rachel trails behind, her hand constantly rubbing the charm bracelet on her wrist. She remembers her grandmother's stories about spirits and curses, the things that lurk in the dark places of the world. She feels her faith wavering, doubts creeping in. Could her prayers really protect her from this? She mutters under her breath, trying to calm herself, but the whispers in the tunnel seem to mock her, growing louder with every step.

Suddenly, the ground beneath them trembles. Rocks dislodge from the walls, clattering onto the ground. A low, rumbling growl fills the tunnel, like the earth itself is angry. Derek's camera screen flickers wildly, and he catches a glimpse of a shadow moving just ahead of them, something shifting in the darkness.

"Did you see that?" he whispers, his voice shaky.

Claire stops, holding up a hand. "Everyone, stay close," she says. "We don't know what's down here."

Eddie shines his flashlight ahead, the beam barely penetrating the thick darkness. "There's something up there," he says, his voice tense. "I don't know what, but... I can feel it watching us."

Rachel's grip on her charm bracelet tightens. "We shouldn't be here," she murmurs, her voice filled with dread. "This place... it's wrong. It feels... evil."

Claire nods, her own fear starting to show. "We have to keep moving," she says. "We're too deep

in to turn back now. Whatever's down here, we need to face it."

They press on, the air growing colder with every step. The whispers around them grow louder, more insistent, mingling with the low rumbling sound that seems to come from the very earth beneath them. The tunnel widens into a larger chamber, the walls covered in strange, ancient symbols carved into the stone.

"What is this place?" Eddie mutters, shining his flashlight on the carvings. The symbols seem to pulse and move, like they're alive. The air feels thick, almost suffocating.

Derek steps closer, his camera capturing everything. "These carvings... they look old. Really old," he says. "Maybe they're some kind of warning?"

Rachel's voice is barely a whisper. "A warning... or a curse."

A sudden, chilling scream echoes through the chamber, a sound that cuts through their souls. It's a woman's scream, filled with pain and fear. The group freezes, their blood running cold.

"Annie?" Claire whispers, her voice trembling.

The scream fades, replaced by a low, mournful wail. The carvings on the walls seem to glow brighter, the air thickening with a sense of impending doom.

"We have to keep going," Eddie says, though his voice is unsteady. "We have to find out what's

happening here."

Section 2: The Trapped Spirits

They move deeper into the chamber, their breaths coming in short, terrified gasps. The air feels electric, as if charged with the emotions of countless lost souls. Rachel notices faint outlines in the moss on the walls — handprints, some large, others small, pressed into the stone. They seem to reach out, desperate, as if trying to escape from some unseen force.

"What are these?" Rachel asks, her voice quivering.

Claire examines them closely, feeling a chill run down her spine. "They're handprints... but they're too perfect, too precise," she says. "Like someone... or something... pressed their hands into the stone."

Derek, always seeking a rational explanation, tries to brush it off. "It could just be the way the moss grew," he suggests, but even he doesn't believe it.

Suddenly, one of the handprints seems to move. The group gasps, stepping back in shock. The handprint begins to twist and contort, the fingers elongating, scraping against the stone with a sound that sets their teeth on edge.

"Oh God," Eddie whispers. "It's alive..."

Before they can react, the handprint pulls free from the wall, and a translucent figure emerges — a woman, her face contorted in agony, her mouth open in a silent scream. She reaches out toward

them, her eyes pleading, as if begging for help.

Rachel lets out a strangled cry, stumbling back. "No... no... this isn't real!"

But Claire steps forward, her heart pounding. "It is real," she says, her voice shaking. "She's a spirit... a lost soul."

The ghostly woman drifts closer, her mouth moving as if speaking, but no sound comes out. Her eyes are wide with fear, and she points frantically toward the deeper part of the chamber, where the darkness is thickest.

Eddie's breath catches in his throat. "She's trying to tell us something," he says. "Something's down there."

Derek adjusts his camera, capturing the apparition. "What do you want us to see?" he asks, more to himself than the ghost.

Suddenly, the spirit's face contorts with a look of sheer terror. She begins to back away, her form flickering like a candle in the wind. The shadows around them grow darker, the air colder, and they hear a low, menacing growl coming from the darkness.

Claire's instincts kick in. "We need to move!" she shouts. "Now!"

They run, their footsteps pounding against the stone floor. The growl grows louder, more guttural, echoing through the tunnel like a monstrous beast chasing them. They don't look back, fear driving them forward.

The tunnel narrows, the walls closing in around them. The growl is right behind them now, so close they can feel its breath on their necks. Claire leads them through a narrow passage, turning sharply, and suddenly, they burst into another chamber, larger and darker than the last.

They come to a stop, panting, their hearts racing. The growl fades, replaced by an eerie silence.

Eddie turns around, his flashlight scanning the room. "Is it gone?" he asks, his voice shaking.

Rachel clutches her charm bracelet, whispering a prayer. "I... I don't know," she murmurs. "I don't think we're safe yet."

Derek checks his camera, relieved to see it's still recording. "Whatever that was... it didn't want us to follow that spirit," he says. "It's trying to keep us away from something."

Claire nods, trying to catch her breath. "We're getting closer to the truth," she says. "Closer than anyone's ever been. And whatever's down here... it doesn't want us to find it."

Section 3: The Hidden Chamber

As they catch their breath, Claire notices a faint light coming from a small opening on the far side of the chamber. "Over there," she says, pointing. "There's a light."

Eddie moves toward the opening, shining his

flashlight inside. "It's a passage," he says. "A small one. We'll have to crawl through."

Rachel's face pales. "I... I don't know if I can do that," she whispers, fear evident in her voice. "I'm claustrophobic."

Claire puts a comforting hand on her shoulder. "You can do this," she says gently. "We're all scared, but we have to stick together."

Derek gives her a reassuring nod. "Yeah, we've got you," he says. "Just take it one step at a time."

Rachel swallows hard, nodding. "Okay... okay, I'll try."

One by one, they crawl through the narrow passage, the walls pressing in on them. The air is stale and cold, and every sound seems amplified

— the scrape of their clothing, the shallow gasps of their breath, the distant dripping of water.

Rachel's hands shake as she crawls, her heart pounding in her chest. She tries to focus

Section 4: The Heart of the Darkness

Rachel's breath comes in short, shallow gasps as she moves forward, forcing herself to keep going despite the oppressive tightness of the tunnel. Each inch feels like a mile, and she can feel the walls pressing closer, the weight of the mountain above them threatening to crush her. Her mind flashes back to childhood, to the time she got trapped in a small closet during a game of hide-and-seek. She remembers the panic, the darkness, the feeling that she would never get out. She pushes the memory down, forcing herself to focus on the here and now, but the fear is almost overwhelming.

Ahead of her, Claire's voice is a steady, calming presence. "You're doing great, Rachel," she calls back. "Just keep moving. We're almost there."

Rachel grits her teeth and keeps crawling, her fingers scraping against the rough stone. The passage seems endless, the darkness swallowing them whole. She can hear Derek behind her, his breathing heavy, his nerves as frayed as hers.

Eddie is at the rear, his flashlight flickering as he moves, the light barely piercing the thick blackness.

Finally, the passage widens, and they emerge into a small, circular chamber. The walls are lined with shelves, filled with objects covered in dust and cobwebs. Strange relics, old books, and odd trinkets fill the space. A single torch, inexplicably lit, casts flickering shadows across the walls. The light is dim and wavering, but it's enough to reveal that they are not alone.

In the center of the chamber stands a figure, a tall, gaunt man with sunken eyes and a face etched with deep lines of age and worry. His clothes are tattered, and he holds a small, leather-bound book

tightly to his chest. His eyes widen with fear as he sees the group.

"Who are you?" Claire demands, stepping forward, her voice steady but cautious. "What are you doing down here?"

The man hesitates, glancing around as if expecting someone or something to appear at any moment. "I'm... I'm Thomas," he stammers, his voice hoarse and cracked, as if he hasn't spoken in years. "I've been trapped down here for... I don't know how long."

Eddie's eyes narrow. "Trapped? By what? Or... by whom?"

Thomas looks down at the book in his hands, his fingers trembling. "By her," he whispers. "By Headless Annie. She's been keeping me here... feeding off my fear, my despair."

Rachel's eyes widen. "Why? Why would she keep you here?"

Thomas swallows hard, glancing nervously at the shadows. "She needs us," he says, his voice barely a whisper. "She needs souls... souls to keep her bound to this place. The more she has, the stronger she becomes. She feeds on our fear, our pain."

Derek takes a cautious step closer. "How did you end up here, Thomas?" he asks. "What happened to you?"

Thomas shudders, clutching the book tighter. "I was a miner," he begins, his voice filled with the weight of years of suffering. "Years ago, I came

down here, chasing the stories, the legends... thinking I could find treasure, something valuable. But what I found... was her. She's not just a ghost. She's something... much worse."

Claire's mind races. "Why didn't you leave? Why stay down here?"

Thomas laughs, a hollow, empty sound. "There's no leaving," he says. "Not once she has you. You become part of her world... part of her curse. I tried to escape, but she always finds me, drags me back. And now... now you're here too."

Section 5: Annie's Curse Revealed

The group falls silent, the weight of Thomas's words settling over them like a dark cloud. They exchange worried glances, unsure of what to do next. Claire steps forward, her voice firm. "We're not going to let her trap us here," she says. "There has to be a way out."

Thomas shakes his head. "You don't understand," he whispers. "She's in control. This place... it's hers. She controls everything that happens down here."

Eddie looks at the strange book Thomas is holding. "What's in that book?" he asks. "Is it important?"

Thomas clutches the book tighter, a look of fear crossing his face. "This... this is her diary," he says, his voice trembling. "It's how I learned about her... her past, her pain. But reading it... it makes her angry. She doesn't want anyone to know."

Rachel takes a step closer, trying to keep her voice calm. "Can we use it?" she asks. "Can it help us break the curse?"

Thomas hesitates, glancing around nervously. "I don't know," he admits. "But it's the only thing I've found that seems to have any power over her. It contains her secrets... her fears. Maybe, just maybe, we can use it against her."

Derek looks at the others, then back at Thomas. "We have to try," he says. "We didn't come all this way to give up now."

Thomas nods slowly, reluctantly handing the book to Claire. "Be careful," he warns. "Every word you read brings you closer to her... brings her closer to you."

Claire opens the book, her hands trembling slightly. The pages are old and brittle, filled with spidery handwriting. The first few pages are filled with stories of Annie's life — a happy childhood, a loving family, a future filled with hope. But as she reads on, the tone shifts, growing darker, filled with anger, fear, and betrayal.

Suddenly, the torch flickers, and the air grows colder. The shadows on the walls seem to grow, twisting and writhing as if alive. A cold breeze sweeps through the chamber, and they hear a faint whisper, growing louder with each passing moment.

"She knows," Thomas whispers, his face pale. "She knows you're reading it."

The whisper becomes a low, menacing growl, echoing through the chamber. The shadows stretch and grow, forming the shape of a woman, her head missing, her body moving with unnatural grace.

The temperature drops even further, and the group shivers, their breath visible in the frigid air.

Eddie steps back, his eyes wide with fear. "She's here," he whispers. "She's coming for us."

Rachel clutches her charm bracelet, muttering a prayer under her breath. "We have to do something," she says, her voice shaking. "We can't just stand here."

Claire's eyes dart across the room, searching for anything they can use. "Keep reading," she says, her voice filled with urgency. "We need to know her story, understand what happened to her."

As Claire continues reading, the growl turns into a scream, a sound filled with pain and rage. The figure in the shadows moves closer, her hand outstretched, reaching for them. The walls shake, the shelves rattling, objects falling to the ground. The book in Claire's hands seems to vibrate, almost as if it's alive.

"Keep going!" Derek shouts, fear in his eyes. "It's our only chance!"

Claire's voice trembles as she reads, her words echoing in the chamber. She reads about Annie's betrayal, her death, and the curse that binds her to Black Mountain. The air grows thicker, the darkness closing in, but she forces herself to keep going.

"Annie," Claire calls out, her voice firm. "We know your story now. We know your pain."

The figure stops, the scream dying in her throat. The shadows seem to hesitate, the growl fading into silence. For a moment, everything is still.

Thomas watches with wide eyes, his hands trembling. "You've done it," he whispers. "You've made her listen."

Claire takes a deep breath, her heart pounding in her chest. "We're not here to hurt you," she says softly. "We're here to help you... to end this curse, once and for all."

The figure in the shadows seems to waver, the darkness shifting. The room grows colder still, but there's a change in the air, a sense of something lifting. The torch flickers, and for a moment, they see her — a woman, her face sad and tired, her eyes filled with tears.

"Please..." she whispers, her voice faint and broken. "Set me free..."

Section 6: Bargaining with the Dead

The chamber falls silent, the air thick with anticipation. The figure of Annie stands before them, her form flickering like a candle in a storm. Her eyes, though shadowed, bore into Claire's with a desperate intensity. For the first time, the group

senses vulnerability in the spirit — a crack in the armor of fury and vengeance that has kept her bound to Black Mountain for so long.

Claire takes a tentative step forward, her voice steady despite the hammering of her heart. "Annie," she says softly, "we know you were wronged. We know you've suffered, but you don't have to keep doing this. Let us help you find peace."

Annie's form wavers, her mouth opening as if to speak, but all that comes out is a hollow, mournful wail that echoes through the chamber. The walls tremble, loose rocks tumbling down, and the group instinctively ducks, shielding their heads. The wail fades into a low, sorrowful whisper.

"She's not convinced," Thomas murmurs, fear lacing his words. "She needs more than words... she needs to feel understood, to feel seen."

Derek nods, his face grim. "We need to show her that we know what she went through... that we feel her pain."

Rachel steps forward, her hands trembling, her eyes filled with determination. "Annie," she says, her voice louder now, carrying over the eerie silence. "We know you lost everything... your family, your future... we've read your story, but we need you to tell us. Tell us in your own words."

The spirit's form wavers again, her eyes narrowing as if considering Rachel's words. The chamber grows colder, frost creeping along the walls, the

breath of each person visible in the icy air. Slowly, painfully, Annie begins to speak. Her voice is thin and cracked, a faint whisper from beyond the grave.

"I was... betrayed," she begins, her tone filled with bitterness. "By those I loved, by those I trusted.

They took everything from me... left me with nothing but my rage and sorrow."

Her words come faster now, pouring out like a river breaking through a dam. She speaks of her life before — a life filled with dreams and love, of a fiancé who promised her the world and then took it away with a lie. She tells of a family that turned their backs on her, of friends who whispered behind her back. She describes her death — the betrayal, the fall, the cold embrace of death on the mountainside.

Claire feels a lump rise in her throat as Annie speaks. She feels the raw emotion, the deep pain that clings to every word. "Annie, we're sorry," she whispers, her voice breaking. "We're so, so sorry."

Annie's eyes flicker to Claire, and for a moment, they soften. "Sorry won't bring me peace," she says, her voice low and trembling. "Sorry won't change what happened. I need... I need..."

"What do you need, Annie?" Eddie asks, his voice gentle. "Tell us. Maybe we can help."

Annie's form shifts again, her head tilting as if she's listening to some distant sound. "I need

justice," she whispers, her voice barely audible. "I need the truth to be known... for them to pay for what they did to me."

Derek looks at the others, his expression serious. "We need to find out who did this to her," he says. "We need to uncover the truth and make sure everyone knows."

Thomas shakes his head slowly, his eyes filled with doubt. "But how?" he asks. "These people are long gone. Their descendants might not even know what their ancestors did."

"We'll find a way," Claire replies firmly. "We have to. It's the only way she'll let us leave this place."

Section 7: Unraveling the Past

The group decides to make their way back to the surface, their minds racing with questions. As they move through the tunnels, they feel Annie's presence all around them, watching, waiting. The cold air nips at their skin, but they push forward, knowing they have a mission — to find the truth about Annie's death and bring justice to her restless spirit.

Once outside, they set up camp and begin to research. Using the notes Thomas has kept over the years and the old books they find in the chamber, they piece together a rough timeline of events leading up to Annie's death. They discover that her fiancé, a man named Jonathan Weaver, had been involved in shady dealings with some of the local miners, promising them a share of a

nonexistent fortune in exchange for favors. When Annie found out, she threatened to expose him, and shortly after, she disappeared.

"Maybe it wasn't just Jonathan," Rachel speculates. "What if there were others involved? Maybe the miners themselves?"

Eddie nods. "We need to find out who else was connected to Jonathan, who stood to gain from Annie's silence."

They split up to search the archives, old newspaper clippings, and historical records. Hours turn into days, and tensions rise as their investigation digs deeper into the past. Claire discovers that Jonathan's family, the Weavers, had been one of the most powerful in the county, with a long history of questionable dealings and a dark reputation among the locals.

"There were always whispers," Thomas tells them, his eyes wide with fear. "Rumors of blackmail, of deals made in the dead of night... if you crossed the Weavers, you didn't live long to tell the tale."

Rachel finds an old letter in the archives, a correspondence between a local judge and Jonathan's father. The letter hints at a cover-up, at something "unfortunate" that needed to be "dealt with quietly." It's enough to convince them that there's more to Annie's story than they first thought.

As they dig further, they start to notice strange occurrences around them. Footsteps echo in the

distance when no one is there. Items disappear and reappear in strange places. The fog seems thicker, more oppressive, as if it's trying to swallow them whole. Annie's presence is growing stronger, more restless.

One night, as they sit around the campfire, Eddie suddenly stiffens, his eyes wide with fear. "Do you hear that?" he whispers.

The others fall silent, straining to listen. At first, there's nothing but the crackling of the fire. Then, faintly, they hear it — a soft, mournful humming, drifting through the trees. It's a woman's voice, carrying a tune that is both haunting and beautiful.

"It's her," Claire breathes. "She's trying to tell us something."

They sit in silence, listening to the eerie melody. The tune is familiar, yet they can't quite place it. Then, suddenly, the humming stops, replaced by a cold, chilling laugh that echoes through the forest. The fire flickers, the shadows dancing wildly around them.

"She's getting impatient," Derek mutters. "We need to move faster."

Section 8: The Pact

The next morning, they decide to visit the old Weaver estate, hoping to find more clues. The house is a crumbling ruin, overgrown with weeds and vines. As they step inside, the air grows colder, and the scent of decay fills their nostrils. The floorboards creak under their weight, and they hear

the faint sound of a piano playing in another room.

"Stay close," Claire warns, her flashlight sweeping across the dusty hallway.

They move through the house, their footsteps echoing in the silence. In the parlor, they find an old, dusty piano, its keys yellowed with age. The lid is open, but there's no one there. The music stops abruptly as they enter, and they feel a chill run down their spines.

"There's something here," Rachel whispers, her eyes darting around the room.

Eddie picks up a photograph from a nearby table. It's a picture of a young man and a woman, smiling at the camera. "That's Jonathan," he says, pointing to the man. "And that must be Annie."

Derek examines the photo closely. "She looks happy," he murmurs. "What happened?"

They continue searching the house, finding more photos, old letters, and documents that paint a picture of a family consumed by greed and corruption. In a hidden compartment in Jonathan's study, they find a small, leather-bound journal. As they flip through the pages, they find entries that confirm their suspicions — Jonathan was planning to betray the miners, and Annie found out.

Suddenly, the temperature drops sharply, and they hear a loud crash from upstairs. They rush up the stairs, their flashlights flickering, to find a mirror shattered, the pieces scattered across the floor. In the broken glass, they see their own reflections,

distorted and twisted.

"She's angry," Derek says, his voice trembling. "She doesn't want us here."

Claire takes a deep breath, steadying herself. "We're close," she says. "We just need to find one more piece of evidence... something that will prove what happened to her."

They search the house, feeling Annie's presence growing stronger with each passing minute. In a hidden drawer, they find a bloodstained letter from Jonathan to his father, confessing his involvement in Annie's death and asking for his father's help to cover it up.

"This is it," Rachel says, holding up the letter. "This is the proof we need."

The house shudders, the walls groaning as if in

agony. A cold wind sweeps through the room, carrying with it the faint scent of earth and decay. The group feels the air tighten around them, like a fist slowly closing.

Claire clutches the letter to her chest, her heart racing. "We have to get out of here," she urges. "This house... it's not safe anymore."

Just as they turn to leave, the doors slam shut with a deafening bang. The windows rattle in their frames, and the temperature drops even further.

Eddie stumbles backward, nearly losing his footing, as a gust of wind slams into him like a physical force.

"She's here," Rachel whispers, eyes wide with fear. "Annie's here."

The shadows around them deepen, coalescing into a darker, denser mass. In the center of the room, a figure begins to materialize — a translucent silhouette with flowing hair and a headless, ghostly form. Annie's presence is palpable, her anger radiating in waves.

"You promised justice," Annie's voice echoes through the room, a chilling whisper that seems to come from everywhere at once. "Show them the truth... or you will not leave this place."

Derek looks around, panicked. "We have the proof! We just need to get it out there," he shouts.

Annie's ghostly form trembles, her headless figure stepping closer. The air thickens, the pressure on their chests growing, as if they're being squeezed by an invisible hand. Claire feels the walls closing in, the room spinning around her.

"We will, Annie!" Claire pleads, clutching the letter. "We'll make sure everyone knows what happened to you. We'll make them remember."

There is a pause, a heartbeat where everything seems to hang in the balance. The wind stops, the house falls silent. Annie's figure wavers, flickers, and then slowly, begins to retreat, fading back into the shadows.

But her voice lingers, a whisper in the cold air. "Do not fail me... or I will find you."

The doors fly open, and the group, still trembling, rushes out of the house into the fog-covered night. Their breaths come in ragged gasps, the reality of what just transpired settling over them like a heavy weight.

"We have to act fast," Eddie pants. "We have to tell the story. Tell everyone. Now."

Claire nods, clutching the letter tightly. "We've got what we need. But we're running out of time."

They glance back at the house, its dark, gaping windows like eyes watching them leave. The shadows shift, and for a moment, they think they see Annie standing there, just watching. Waiting.

They pile into their vehicle, hearts pounding, and start the drive back down the mountain, determined to bring Annie's story to light — to finally bring her the justice that will set her free... if they can survive long enough to do it.

But as they descend, the fog thickens once more, swallowing the road ahead. A low, mournful hum begins to drift through the trees again, growing louder, more insistent. The group shares a nervous glance.

Because now, they know: Annie is not done with them yet.

Chapter 6: Echoes in the Darkness Section 1: The Descent Begins

The fog wraps around their vehicle like a thick, suffocating blanket as they make their way down

Black Mountain. The headlights cut through the mist in weak, pale beams, and the road ahead is barely visible. Derek grips the steering wheel with white-knuckled intensity, his eyes darting back and forth as if anticipating something to jump out of the dark at any moment. The tension in the car is palpable; every creak and groan of the vehicle feels like an ominous warning.

Eddie, sitting in the backseat, keeps glancing over his shoulder, his paranoia spiking with each passing minute. "I swear... I feel like she's still with us," he mutters under his breath. "Like she's watching us... waiting."

"Keep it together, Eddie," Claire says, though her voice is shaky. She clutches the leather-bound journal they found in the old Weaver estate. "We have the proof. All we have to do is get this to the authorities, to the media... anyone who will listen. We're almost there."

Rachel sits in the passenger seat, her hands trembling slightly. She glances at Derek. "How much further?"

"Shouldn't be long now," Derek replies, his voice tense. But even as he says it, the fog thickens, the road seeming to stretch out endlessly in front of

them, as if they are driving in circles. He tries to steady his breathing, feeling a cold sweat trickle down the back of his neck.

Suddenly, the radio crackles to life, a burst of static cutting through the thick silence in the car. The white noise grows louder, more aggressive, before a faint, ghostly voice breaks through.

"She's... here... still here..." the voice whispers, sending chills down everyone's spine.

Derek instinctively slams his foot on the brake, and the car skids to a stop, the tires screeching against the wet asphalt. "What the hell was that?" he exclaims, his heart pounding in his chest.

"It's her," Eddie breathes, panic rising in his voice. "Annie... she's in the car with us!"

Rachel grabs the radio dial and twists it, but the voice only grows louder, more insistent. "You promised... you promised me..." the voice murmurs, sending a shiver through everyone's bones.

The fog outside swirls and thickens, pressing against the windows like something alive, trying to get in. Claire's breathing quickens. "We need to keep moving. We need to get out of here, now!"

Derek nods, and with a shaky hand, he presses the accelerator. The car lurches forward, but the fog only seems to grow denser, more suffocating. The headlights flicker, the engine sputters.

"Come on," Derek mutters, gripping the wheel tighter. "Come on..."

The road twists and turns in unexpected ways, curves that weren't there before seem to stretch out, twisting in on themselves like a snake. "Is it just me, or is the road changing?" Rachel asks, her voice tinged with fear.

Eddie looks out the window and sees the outlines of trees moving, shifting like shadows against the fog. "No... it's not just you," he says, his voice almost a whisper. "Something's... playing with us."

Section 2: The Spirit's Wrath

A sudden, sharp knock on the window startles everyone. Derek nearly loses control of the wheel, swerving back onto the narrow road. The fog outside seems to pulse with a malevolent energy. Another knock, louder this time. Rachel turns and gasps; a pale handprint is visible on the passenger window, as if pressed from the outside.

"Drive faster!" Claire shouts, feeling a surge of panic. "Don't stop for anything!"

Derek's foot presses harder on the accelerator, but the car seems to be fighting against him, the engine groaning under the strain. Eddie is muttering a prayer under his breath, his eyes squeezed shut. "Please... please let us get out of here," he repeats.

The knocking comes again, but this time, it's accompanied by a cold, disembodied laugh that echoes through the car. The windows fog up from the inside, and frost begins to creep along the glass, forming patterns that look disturbingly like faces, screaming in silent agony.

"She's angry," Rachel whispers, clutching her arms. "She knows we found out the truth... she's not going to let us leave that easily."

Suddenly, the car jerks violently, as if it hit something. Derek slams on the brakes again, the vehicle skidding to a halt. They all stare ahead, their breath caught in their throats.

There, standing in the middle of the road, is a headless figure in white. Annie. She is holding something — a severed head in her hands, her fingers wrapped tightly around its hair. The head turns, and they recognize the face. It's Jonathan Weaver, his eyes wide with terror, his mouth frozen in a silent scream.

"No... no, no, no," Eddie gasps, his heart racing. "This isn't happening..."

Annie's figure begins to advance toward them, slowly, methodically. Derek tries to start the car again, but the engine only sputters and dies. "Come on!" he shouts, frantically turning the key. "Come on!"

The temperature inside the car drops even further. Their breath is visible in the icy air. The frost creeps faster across the windows, obscuring their view. The radio crackles to life again, the same ghostly voice echoing through the static.

"You promised... justice... truth..." it whispers.

Claire, feeling desperation take over, grabs the journal from the backseat. "We have what you

want, Annie! We have the proof! Let us go, and we'll make sure everyone knows what happened to you!"

Annie's figure stops, standing motionless in the road, her headless body swaying slightly. Then, slowly, she raises the severed head in her hands, and the mouth begins to move.

"She... lies..." Jonathan's voice rasps from the disembodied head. "They lie..."

The head's eyes snap open, staring directly at them, filled with a deep, unnatural malice.

Section 3: The Path of Nightmares

Without warning, the fog outside the car swirls violently, and they feel a sudden jolt as if the car has been pushed. The vehicle lurches forward down a slope they hadn't seen, careening wildly. Derek wrestles with the steering wheel, trying to regain control, but it feels as if invisible hands are guiding them, steering them deeper into the darkness.

"Brace yourselves!" he shouts, and they all hold on as the car speeds down the narrow, twisting path, barely avoiding trees and rocks that seem to jump out at them.

The laughter returns, louder this time, mingled with the sounds of a chorus of whispers, voices all around them. The fog is alive with shapes and shadows, flickering figures darting through the mist. Rachel turns to see a face pressed against the rear window — a face she recognizes from the old

photographs in the Weaver estate.

"Annie!" she cries out, but the figure vanishes in a blink, replaced by another, and then another. The fog thickens even more, and the air grows colder still, freezing their breath in midair.

The road straightens suddenly, and they find themselves driving past familiar landmarks — the twisted oak, the old miner's cabin — but they've been driving in the opposite direction. The path loops back on itself, leading them in circles.

"This can't be happening," Derek mutters, a tremor in his voice. "We've passed that tree three times now."

"She's trapping us," Eddie says, his eyes wide. "She's making us relive the night over and over again... just like she did."

Claire's eyes widen with realization. "We're caught in her loop... the same one that keeps her spirit bound to this place."

They hear a low rumbling sound from behind, like thunder rolling through the mountains. The fog parts just enough for them to see headlights in the distance, rapidly approaching. "Another car?" Derek says, squinting into the mist.

But then, a horrible realization dawns on them — the headlights are coming toward them on the same narrow path. "No, it's us," Rachel whispers, horrified. "It's our own car."

The two sets of headlights grow closer, merging in the fog. Just as they are about to collide, the path

splits, and they veer onto a different road, a road none of them had seen before. It's narrow and covered in jagged rocks, leading steeply uphill.

Section 4: Confronting the Past

At the top of the hill, they see the outline of an old church, its windows broken, its steeple leaning precariously to one side. "We have to go there," Claire says, her voice urgent. "Maybe we can find something that will help us break this loop."

They exit the car cautiously, feeling the thick fog swirl around their ankles. The air is cold and heavy, filled with the scent of wet earth and decaying leaves. As they approach the church, they hear the faint sound of chanting coming from within, a low, rhythmic murmur that grows louder with each step.

Derek pushes the creaky door open, and they step inside. The interior is dark, the only light coming from a few flickering candles on the altar. The candles cast eerie shadows that dance along the cracked walls, creating shapes that seem to move on their own. The air inside is thick with the smell of old wood and damp stone. As they move deeper into the church, the chanting grows louder, a chorus of disembodied voices rising and falling in a strange, unsettling rhythm.

Rachel steps closer to the altar and sees something carved into the wood — a series of symbols, ancient and indecipherable, but pulsing faintly as if alive. "What is this?" she whispers, reaching out to touch them.

Claire stops her. "Don't... it could be some sort of trap."

But it's too late. As Rachel's fingers graze the carvings, the room shudders, and the ground beneath them trembles violently. The chanting stops abruptly, replaced by a deafening silence.

Then, a voice — low, raspy, filled with centuries of sorrow and rage — echoes through the darkened space.

"You cannot leave... until justice is done."

The church door slams shut behind them with a bone-rattling crash, and the room plunges into darkness. Shadows stretch and twist along the walls, and a cold wind sweeps through, blowing out the candles. The temperature drops sharply, and the sound of footsteps echoes through the nave

— slow, deliberate, coming closer.

Derek spins around, trying to see through the darkness. "Annie?" he calls out, his voice cracking with fear. "Is that you?"

A figure emerges from the shadows, slowly taking shape. It's Annie, her headless form moving toward them, her hands outstretched. In one hand, she holds the severed head of Jonathan Weaver; in the other, a long, rusted chain. Her presence fills the room with a bone-chilling cold, and her voice — that voice — cuts through the darkness like a knife.

"Find the truth... or be lost... forever."

And with that, the church begins to shake, the

walls closing in as the group realizes they have only one chance left: to confront the past, uncover the hidden secrets that bind Annie to this place, and somehow, find a way to escape her wrath before they, too, become part of the legend of Black Mountain.

CHAPTER 7: INTO THE ABYSS

Section 1: The Church of Shadows

The walls of the old church creak and groan like the ribs of some dying creature. The darkness inside is suffocating, closing in on them with every second. Claire's heart pounds in her chest as she grips the journal tightly, the ancient carvings on the altar still glowing faintly with a sickly, greenish light. She can barely see her friends, the shadows swallowing them whole. Only Annie's headless figure remains clear, moving ever closer, dragging that rusted chain behind her, scraping along the floor like a whisper of doom.

Rachel feels the walls press against her shoulders, the air growing thick and cold. She steps back, her breath quick and shallow. "We need to find a way out," she says, panic tightening her throat. "We can't stay here. She'll kill us!"

Eddie nods, his eyes wide with fear. He can barely keep his hands from trembling. "How? The door's

locked, and the windows... they're barred shut. We're trapped."

Derek, still clutching the flashlight, swings its beam around the room. The light catches on something glinting in the corner — a narrow set of steps leading down into the ground. "A cellar," he mutters. "Maybe there's another way out down there."

Claire steps forward, her voice firm despite the terror gripping her heart. "It's our only chance. We have to try."

The chanting resumes, louder this time, the voices blending together into a deafening cacophony.

Annie's headless figure begins to sway, as if caught in some invisible wind, and she lets out a low, guttural growl. The chain she holds begins to rattle, vibrating with a dark energy.

"Run!" Derek shouts, and they bolt for the stairs.

They descend quickly into the cellar, the air growing colder with each step. The steps are narrow and uneven, slick with moisture. The deeper they go, the more the darkness thickens, becoming almost tangible, like a weight pressing down on them. At the bottom, they find themselves in a narrow stone corridor, the walls lined with old, rotting wooden beams.

The flashlight flickers, casting long, distorted shadows along the walls. "What is this place?" Eddie whispers, his voice barely audible over the sound of their breathing.

Rachel looks around, her eyes wide. "It feels... ancient. Like it's been here for centuries."

They hear a faint sound, like a whisper, coming from deeper within the corridor. "We have to keep moving," Claire says. "We need to find a way out before she follows us down here."

They move cautiously through the corridor, the flashlight flickering in Derek's hand. The walls seem to close in around them, the ceiling low and oppressive. Strange symbols are carved into the stone, similar to those on the altar upstairs, their shapes twisted and alien. Claire reaches out to touch one, feeling the cold stone beneath her fingers, and a shiver runs down her spine.

"Do you think these symbols have something to do with Annie?" Rachel asks, her voice echoing in the narrow space.

"I don't know," Claire replies, her hand lingering on the carving. "But I think they're a clue... something to do with how she's trapped here."

Suddenly, they hear a low, rumbling sound from behind them — the sound of heavy footsteps, slowly descending the stairs. They freeze, turning to look back the way they came. The footsteps grow louder, closer, and then they hear the unmistakable sound of the chain dragging along the stone steps.

"She's coming," Eddie breathes, his face pale. "We have to go, now!"

Section 2: The Hidden Crypt

They rush down the corridor, their footsteps echoing through the stone passageway. The air grows colder still, each breath like a puff of mist. The flashlight flickers again, and Derek shakes it desperately. "Don't you dare die on me now," he mutters.

The corridor opens up into a larger chamber, the ceiling high and vaulted. In the center of the room stands an old, crumbling statue of a woman in flowing robes, her face obscured by years of decay. At her feet, a large stone slab is set into the ground, covered in dust and cobwebs.

Claire moves closer, wiping away the dust with her sleeve. Carved into the stone is an inscription, barely legible in the dim light:

"Here lies she who knows the secrets of the mountain, bound by chains of vengeance and blood."

Rachel steps back, a chill running through her. "What does that mean?"

"It's a burial site," Claire says, her voice tight with fear. "A crypt... but for who?"

Before anyone can answer, a gust of cold wind sweeps through the chamber, and they hear a faint whisper, almost inaudible. Claire's eyes widen. "Did you hear that?"

They all nod, their eyes darting around the dark room. The whisper grows louder, more distinct, until they can make out words:

"Set... me... free..."

Derek shines the flashlight around, and the beam falls on a narrow tunnel leading deeper into the ground. "Maybe we're not alone down here," he says, swallowing hard.

"Or maybe it's Annie," Eddie adds, fear making his voice tremble. "Playing tricks on us."

Claire takes a deep breath. "Either way, we need to keep moving. We have to find a way out of this place."

They enter the tunnel, the walls closing in even more, the ceiling so low they have to crouch. The air is stale and thick with the scent of decay. They hear the sound of water dripping somewhere in the distance, the only noise in the oppressive silence.

Rachel starts to feel a tightness in her chest, her breathing becoming labored. "I don't like this... I feel like I'm being suffocated," she gasps.

"Just keep moving," Claire urges, trying to keep her own fear in check. "We're almost there."

But the tunnel twists and turns, leading them deeper and deeper underground. The walls begin to close in even more, the space growing narrower with each step. Derek has to turn sideways to squeeze through, his shoulders brushing against the cold, damp stone.

They hear a faint, distant noise — a sound like crying, echoing through the tunnel. Claire stops, straining to listen. "Do you hear that?" she asks.

The others nod, their faces pale with fear. The crying grows louder, more desperate, and they

realize it's coming from behind them.

"Go!" Derek shouts, and they push forward, moving as quickly as they can through the narrow space. The crying turns into a wail, a sound of pure agony that seems to fill the tunnel, reverberating through their bones.

The flashlight flickers again, and Derek slaps it against his palm. The light steadies for a moment, but then goes out completely, plunging them into total darkness.

Section 3: Confronting the Spirits

They are blind in the darkness, feeling their way along the damp, cold walls. Panic sets in as they hear the wailing grow louder, closer, surrounding them from all sides. Eddie feels something brush against his arm and jumps back with a scream. "What was that?!"

"I don't know!" Claire replies, trying to keep her voice steady. "Just keep moving!"

But the tunnel seems to go on forever, the darkness pressing down on them. Rachel's breath comes in quick, shallow gasps. "I can't breathe," she whispers, panic rising in her chest. "I can't... I can't..."

Derek reaches out and grabs her hand. "Hold on, Rachel. We're going to get out of this. Just keep moving, okay?"

They push forward, the air growing colder still. They hear footsteps behind them, slow and deliberate, echoing off the stone walls. The crying

turns into laughter, a high, chilling sound that makes their skin crawl.

Eddie turns around, his back against the wall. "Annie, stop this!" he shouts into the darkness. "We're trying to help you!"

The laughter stops abruptly, replaced by a deep, resonant voice that fills the tunnel. "You cannot help... only suffer..."

The ground beneath them suddenly trembles, and they feel a deep rumbling beneath their feet. Dust falls from the ceiling, and the walls seem to shift, closing in even more.

"We need light!" Claire shouts. "Derek, do you have a lighter?"

Derek fumbles in his pocket and pulls out a small lighter, flicking it open. A tiny flame flickers in the darkness, casting a dim light around them. They see the narrow walls, the dirt and grime, and the symbols carved into the stone — symbols that seem to glow with a faint, eerie light.

"What do they mean?" Rachel asks, her voice barely above a whisper.

"I don't know," Claire replies, staring at the symbols. "But they're not natural... they're not right..."

Suddenly, the ground shakes again, more violently this time. The walls crack, and they hear the sound of stones shifting, falling. The tunnel begins to collapse around them.

"Run!" Derek shouts, and they bolt forward, the lighter flickering in his hand. The walls close in, and they feel the earth shift beneath their feet, the sound of crumbling stone all around them.

They burst into a larger chamber just as the tunnel behind them collapses completely. Dust fills the air, and they cough, waving their hands to clear it away.

Section 4: The Heart of the Mountain

In the center of the chamber stands an old, ornate mirror, its glass fogged and cracked, the frame covered in strange carvings similar to those they had seen upstairs in the church and throughout the tunnels. The mirror seems to pulse with a faint, otherworldly glow, as if it is alive — as if it is watching them.

"What... is that?" Eddie whispers, stepping back, his eyes wide with fear.

Rachel feels an unnatural pull toward the mirror, like an invisible hand reaching out, tugging at her very soul. "I don't know," she mutters, almost in a trance, taking a step closer. "But I think... I think it wants us to come closer."

Claire moves beside her, gripping her arm. "No, Rachel. Stay back. We don't know what it is, or what it could do."

Derek steps closer to the mirror, lifting the lighter to get a better look. The flickering flame casts strange, dancing shadows across the cracked glass.

"It looks old... really old," he says. "And it's covered in those symbols again."

He reaches out, his fingers hovering just inches from the surface of the mirror. "Don't touch it!" Claire yells, but it's too late — Derek's fingertips make contact with the glass.

A shock of cold runs through Derek's hand, freezing his fingers in place. The mirror begins to ripple, like water disturbed by a pebble, and the symbols carved into the frame start to glow brighter, bathing the room in an eerie green light.

Derek tries to pull his hand away, but he can't move. "I'm stuck!" he cries out, panic rising in his voice. "It's got me!"

The glass of the mirror swirls, and within its depths, an image begins to form — a dark, wooded path, shrouded in fog. Slowly, a figure emerges from the mist — Annie, headless, her dress tattered and stained, holding her severed head in her hands.

She turns her head toward them, and they see her eyes — hollow, filled with an unending sorrow and rage. Her mouth moves, but no words come out.

Instead, they hear her voice in their minds, a whisper that sends chills down their spines:

"Find... the truth... or be bound... to this place... forever..."

Suddenly, the chamber grows colder still, the temperature dropping rapidly. Frost forms on the walls, their breath misting in the air. The mirror begins to hum with a low, resonant vibration, the

light pulsing brighter with each second.

"Derek, pull back!" Eddie shouts, rushing forward to grab his friend's arm. "We need to break the connection!"

Claire grabs a rock from the floor and raises it above her head, ready to smash the mirror. "We have to destroy it!" she yells. "It's the source of her power — it's keeping her here!"

"No!" a voice booms from the mirror, deep and commanding. "Do not break the seal! Or you will unleash... something far worse..."

Claire hesitates, the rock still held above her head. "What do you mean?" she demands. "Who are you?"

The voice sighs, a long, mournful sound. "I am... the keeper of the mountain. I am bound here, as she is. But if you destroy the mirror... you will unleash the darkness that sleeps beneath..."

"Annie?" Rachel whispers, staring at the image in the mirror. "Is this you? Are you speaking through it?"

The figure in the mirror shakes its head slowly. "I am... her jailer. I keep her here, to protect the world above... from the darkness below. She is but a guardian... a warning... to those who seek the truth."

Derek, his hand still stuck to the mirror, winces as pain shoots through his arm. "Then tell us!" he shouts, desperate. "What truth? What do we need to do?"

The voice falls silent for a moment, as if considering their plea. Then it speaks again, softer this time, almost compassionate. "Find the one who betrayed her... the one who set her fate in motion. Only then... will the curse be lifted."

The mirror begins to glow brighter, the light blinding, and then — suddenly — it shatters, exploding outward with a deafening crash. Derek is thrown back, hitting the ground hard, his hand free at last but bleeding from dozens of tiny cuts. The shards of glass scatter across the chamber, and the eerie green light fades, plunging them into darkness once more.

Section 5: The Betrayer's Name

Rachel rushes to Derek's side, helping him sit up. "Are you okay?" she asks, her voice thick with worry.

Derek nods, wincing as he flexes his hand. "I think so... but what the hell was that?"

Claire looks at the shattered glass, pieces still glowing faintly in the dark. "The one who betrayed her... that's who we need to find. It's the key to everything."

"But who could it be?" Eddie asks, his voice tense. "That was over a hundred years ago, right? How are we supposed to find out who betrayed her?"

Claire thinks back to the journal she found, flipping through the pages in her mind. "Maybe it's in the records... the journal. There was a section about Annie's life before she died. If we

can find out who she was close to, who had reason to betray her..."

Rachel nods. "It's a start. But we need to get out of here first. The tunnel's collapsed, but maybe there's another way."

They start to search the chamber, feeling along the walls for any sign of a hidden passage or another exit. As they do, they hear a soft, rhythmic sound

— a faint heartbeat, growing louder with each step.

"Do you hear that?" Eddie asks, turning his head.

"Yeah... it's coming from behind the statue," Claire says, moving toward the old, crumbling figure. She reaches out, touching the base, and feels a slight vibration. "There's something here..."

She presses against the statue, and it moves slightly, grinding against the stone floor. Derek and Eddie join her, pushing harder, and the statue slowly slides to the side, revealing a narrow staircase descending further into the darkness.

"This must be it," Derek says, his voice filled with a mix of fear and determination. "The way out... or deeper in."

Rachel swallows hard, her hand gripping Derek's tightly. "I don't know if I want to find out what's down there," she whispers.

"We have no choice," Claire says, taking the first step down. "If we want to survive... if we want to end this... we have to keep going."

They descend the staircase, each step echoing through the stone walls. The heartbeat grows louder, more insistent, and they feel it pulsing through the ground beneath them. The air grows colder still, their breath visible in the dim light.

At the bottom of the stairs, they find themselves in a small, circular chamber, the walls covered in ancient symbols and strange, twisted carvings. In the center of the room is a stone pedestal, and atop it, a single book — old, leather-bound, its cover worn and faded.

Claire approaches it cautiously, her hand hovering over the cover. "This must be it... the answer," she murmurs, then opens the book, flipping through the pages quickly. She finds a passage, written in a shaky, faded script:

"To bind her, they betrayed her with false promises and cruel lies. Her name was given in trust, but broken by the one she loved most... Jonathan Weaver."

"Jonathan Weaver?" Rachel asks, confused. "Who is he?"

Claire's eyes widen. "He was... Annie's fiancé. They were supposed to marry, but he vanished... and now he's the one she holds in her head..."

The air grows colder still, the light flickering. They hear a whisper, faint and filled with pain:

"Find... him..."

Annie's headless form begins to appear again, her figure faintly glowing in the dark, her severed head

held tightly in her hand. The group steps back, their hearts racing.

"We have to find his grave," Derek says, gripping the book tightly. "That's where it started... and that's where it has to end."

As they turn to leave the chamber, the ground begins to tremble again, and they hear Annie's voice, soft but commanding:

"Hurry... before... it's too late..."

They race back up the stairs, the sound of the heartbeat echoing in their ears, knowing that time is running out — that they must find the truth, or be lost forever in the depths of Black Mountain, just like the many souls who vanished before them.

Chapter 8: The Truth Beneath the Surface Part 1: The Haunting Echo

The air is heavy with tension as they emerge from the dark, winding staircase. Rachel, Derek, Claire, and Eddie step back into the gloomy church, each feeling the oppressive weight of the darkness pressing down on them. The cold is sharper now, almost unbearable, and they can see their breath puffing out in white clouds. Annie's warning rings in their ears: *"Hurry... before... it's too late..."*

Claire clutches the ancient journal against her chest, her fingers trembling slightly. "We need to find Jonathan Weaver's grave," she insists, her voice laced with urgency. "It's the only way to

break this curse."

Derek nods, still shaken from his contact with the mirror. "But where do we even begin? This place is a maze."

Rachel looks around, trying to gather her thoughts. Her own fear is palpable, but she knows they can't afford to waste any time. "The graveyard," she says finally. "There was one behind the church... maybe he's buried there."

Eddie's flashlight flickers, casting long, jagged shadows across the decrepit walls. "Let's move," he mutters, pushing open the warped wooden door that leads outside. The hinges creak loudly, as if protesting against the effort.

As they step out into the night, a thick fog has settled over the mountainside, swirling around them like a living entity. The graveyard looms ahead, its headstones barely visible in the murky darkness. A gust of wind blows through, carrying with it the faint scent of decaying leaves and earth.

Rachel shivers, gripping Derek's arm tightly. "Do you feel that?" she whispers. "It's like... we're being watched."

Claire nods, her eyes scanning the fog for any sign of movement. "Annie isn't the only spirit here," she says, her voice low. "The keeper of the mountain... the darkness beneath... there are others trapped in this place."

They move cautiously through the fog, their footsteps crunching on the gravel path that winds

through the old cemetery. The headstones are cracked and covered in moss, some leaning precariously, others barely legible. The fog seems to thicken with each step, swallowing their light and muting their voices.

Eddie stops suddenly, his eyes fixed on something in the distance. "There!" he points, his hand trembling. "Do you see it?"

They all turn to look and see a tall, thin figure standing at the far end of the graveyard. It is shrouded in fog, its features obscured, but they can feel its gaze upon them — a cold, penetrating stare that sends a chill down their spines.

"Is it... Jonathan?" Rachel asks, her voice quavering.

The figure doesn't move, but the fog around it seems to pulse, as if alive. Derek takes a step forward, gripping the flashlight tightly. "We need to find out," he says, his voice tense. "If it's him... maybe he can tell us what happened."

As they approach, the figure begins to fade, dissolving into the mist. A low, mournful wail echoes through the cemetery, like a whisper carried on the wind. The ground trembles beneath their feet, and they feel a cold, damp hand brush against their ankles, as if reaching up from the grave itself.

"Run!" Claire shouts, grabbing Rachel's arm and pulling her back. They sprint through the graveyard, dodging the headstones and broken markers, the fog swirling around them like a living

entity. They hear footsteps behind them — fast, relentless — but when they glance back, there is nothing but mist and shadows.

Finally, they reach a large, ornate headstone near the center of the cemetery. It is newer than the others, the name *Jonathan Weaver* carved deeply into the stone. The ground beneath it seems disturbed, as if recently dug up and then covered again in haste.

"This is it," Claire pants, bending over to catch her breath. "We found it…"

Derek drops to his knees, pulling out a small folding shovel from his backpack. "We have to dig," he says, his voice firm. "We need to see what's inside."

Rachel hesitates, her eyes wide with fear. "Are you sure? What if we release something worse?"

"We don't have a choice," Eddie says, grabbing another shovel and starting to dig. "Annie told us to find him… this has to be it."

As they dig, the ground seems to resist them, the dirt heavy and cold, almost like cement. The fog presses in closer, the temperature dropping further with every shovelful of earth they remove. They work in silence, their breaths coming in short gasps, the only sound the scraping of metal against stone.

Suddenly, Claire's shovel hits something hard — a dull, hollow thud. "I've got something," she says, excitement and fear mixing in her voice. They dig

faster, uncovering the top of a wooden coffin, its surface cracked and rotting.

"Open it," Derek says, his voice tight with fear. "We have to see."

They pry open the coffin lid, and a foul stench fills the air — the smell of decay and death. Inside, they see a skeleton, its bones bleached white, wearing tattered clothes. Clutched in its bony hand is a small, leather-bound book.

Claire reaches in, her hand trembling, and takes the book. "This must be it… his journal."

As she opens the book, a cold wind howls through the graveyard, and the ground begins to shake violently. The fog thickens, swirling into a vortex around them. From the depths of the mist, they hear a voice — low, raspy, filled with sorrow and anger:

"Who... dares... disturb... my rest?"

Part 2: Jonathan's Tale

Claire holds the journal tightly, flipping through its fragile pages as the voice grows louder, filling the air with a bone-chilling resonance. The fog closes in around them, and they feel the cold seeping into their bones, their breath turning into icy mist.

"Jonathan Weaver," Claire whispers, "we seek the truth of what happened to Annie. We seek to end the curse that binds this place."

The wind howls in response, but then the voice softens, as if considering her words. "Annie... she

was my love, my light," the voice whispers. "But I was a fool... a coward..."

The journal in Claire's hands begins to glow faintly, the ink shimmering on the old pages. She starts to read aloud, her voice steady despite the fear gripping her heart:

"September 2, 1895. The mountain air is cold tonight, and I feel its chill deep within my bones. I have made a terrible mistake... one that I fear cannot be undone. I promised Annie a life of happiness, of love... but I betrayed her. I chose power over love, ambition over truth."

As she reads, the fog around them seems to part slightly, revealing fleeting images — glimpses of a bygone era. They see a young couple, Annie and Jonathan, laughing together by a stream, holding hands under the autumn leaves. Then, the images shift — Annie standing alone, looking lost and betrayed, while Jonathan is seen in secret meetings with shadowy figures.

"I thought I could control it," the journal continues, "the darkness beneath the mountain. I thought I could harness its power... but I was wrong. The pact I made... it was with forces beyond our world, forces that cannot be bound by mortal hands. And now... I have condemned us all."

Rachel shudders as the images change again — now showing a ritual, Jonathan standing before an altar deep within a cave, chanting words in an ancient, forbidden language. The darkness around

him seems to pulse, alive and hungry.

"When Annie found out... she tried to stop me," the journal reads. "She begged me to leave, to break the pact. But I could not... I was too far gone. In my desperation, I... I betrayed her. I handed her over to them, thinking they would spare me. But they did not. They bound her spirit to this mountain, to guard the darkness forever."

The ground trembles beneath them, and they hear Annie's voice, faint but clear, filled with pain and betrayal: "Jonathan... why?"

Tears sting Claire's eyes as she continues, "He used her, didn't he? He traded her soul to keep himself alive... or to gain something more."

A sudden flash of light, bright and searing, fills the grave-yard, and for a moment, they are blinded.

When their vision clears, they see the figure of Jonathan standing before them — his face gaunt, eyes hollow, his expression a mix of sorrow and regret.

"I never meant for this," Jonathan's ghostly form says, his voice thick with emotion. "I was a fool... I thought I could control the darkness. But I loved her... I swear I loved her."

"You betrayed her!" Rachel cries, stepping forward, her voice breaking. "You left her to suffer... to be a warning to all who come here!"

Jonathan hangs his head, his form flickering like a dying flame. "I know... I know... and I have been trapped here ever since, bound by my own sins.

But you... you have a chance to end it. You must sever the connection between her and the darkness... break the pact I made."

"How?" Eddie demands. "Tell us how!"

Jonathan's form grows fainter, his voice softer. "Her remains... they must be burned...

Jonathan's form grows fainter, his voice softer. "Her remains... they must be burned in the fire of the mountain's heart. Only then will she be free. But beware... the darkness will not let her go easily. It will fight back... it will try to claim more souls to feed its hunger."

His form flickers one last time, his eyes pleading. "Do what I could not... save her... save yourselves..."

With that, Jonathan's ghostly image dissipates into the fog, leaving the group standing alone in the graveyard, the oppressive silence settling around them like a shroud.

Part 3: Descent into Darkness

Derek exhales, looking around at the others. "So, we need to find her remains and burn them in the mountain's heart. But where do we even start?"

Claire, her face pale but determined, clutches the journal. "He mentioned a cave... an altar deep within it. That must be where he made the pact and where her spirit is bound."

Rachel nods. "We need to find that cave, then. But how do we locate it?"

Eddie scans the fog-covered graveyard. "It has to be somewhere nearby. Jonathan wouldn't have been able to go far with Annie... and if the darkness is bound to that spot, it's where we need to be."

They hear a rustling behind them, and all four of them spin around, flashlights shining into the thick fog. The mist parts briefly, revealing the shadowy outline of a path leading away from the graveyard and into the woods. The air grows colder, and they feel the hairs on the back of their necks stand up.

Claire takes a deep breath. "That's our way in. It has to be."

They begin to walk down the path, their footsteps crunching on the dead leaves. The fog seems to grow thicker with every step, the darkness closing in around them. The wind howls through the trees, carrying with it faint, mournful cries that make their skin crawl.

As they move deeper into the woods, the air becomes dense and heavy, almost suffocating. Branches reach out like skeletal fingers, snagging at their clothes, and the ground becomes uneven, slippery with mud and moss. Derek stumbles, catching himself just before falling, his heart racing.

"We have to be careful," he mutters. "This place is trying to keep us out."

Rachel steps forward, her expression resolute. "We have to keep going. Annie's counting on us."

They push on, the path winding through the dense forest, leading them further away from the church and deeper into the heart of Black Mountain. The air is colder now, their breaths visible in the dim light, and the fog swirls around their feet like a living thing.

Eddie points ahead. "Look... there's something up there."

They see the faint outline of a cave entrance, half- hidden behind a curtain of overgrown vines and thick, twisted tree roots. A cold breeze emanates from within, carrying with it the unmistakable scent of damp earth and decay.

Claire nods, tightening her grip on the journal. "This must be it... the cave."

Rachel steps closer, her flashlight beam piercing the darkness just enough to reveal the opening. "If Jonathan's journal is right, this is where we need to go."

They hesitate for a moment, the weight of what lies ahead heavy on their minds. Then, with a silent agreement, they step forward and enter the cave.

Inside, the darkness is absolute, their flashlights barely making a dent in the inky blackness. The air is thick with moisture, and they can hear the distant drip of water echoing off the stone walls.

The path is narrow, forcing them to walk in single file, their shoulders brushing against the cold, damp rock.

The deeper they go, the more oppressive the atmosphere becomes. The walls seem to close in on them, and the sounds grow louder — whispers, faint and unintelligible, echoing all around them. The ground beneath their feet feels uneven, almost alive, shifting with every step.

They come to a fork in the cave — one path leading down into the earth, the other veering sharply to the left. Rachel turns to Claire. "Which way?"

Claire flips through the journal, scanning the pages by the dim flashlight. "He said... down. To the heart of the mountain."

Derek nods. "Then that's where we go."

They take the downward path, descending deeper and deeper into the cave. The temperature drops even further, their breaths forming clouds of vapor in the dim light. The walls are covered in strange markings, symbols that seem to writhe and shift when looked at directly.

The whispers grow louder, more insistent. They sound like a chorus of voices, crying out in pain, anger, and fear. Rachel shivers, her hand brushing against the rough stone wall. "I don't like this... it feels like the walls are closing in."

Eddie, ever the skeptic, mutters, "Just keep moving. We have to get to the bottom of this."

As they descend, the ground becomes slippery with moisture, and they have to move carefully to avoid falling. The air grows colder still, their

breath coming in short, sharp bursts. The darkness seems to throb around them, like a living, breathing thing.

Finally, they reach a wide chamber at the bottom of the cave. The walls are covered in strange, glowing symbols, pulsating with a faint, eerie light. In the center of the chamber is a stone altar, stained with dark, dried blood. Above it hangs a heavy iron chain, its links rusted and ancient.

On the altar lies a pile of bones, small and fragile, covered in a thin layer of dust. A ragged white dress lies draped over them, stained with dirt and blood. The air around the altar is thick with a palpable sense of dread, and they feel a pressure building in their chests, making it hard to breathe.

Derek steps forward, his voice a whisper. "This... this must be Annie."

Rachel nods, her eyes wide with fear. "But where's the fire? How do we burn her remains here?"

Claire takes a step closer, her eyes fixed on the altar. "There's something written here... on the stone." She bends down, brushing the dust away to reveal a carved inscription in an ancient, unreadable script.

Suddenly, the chamber is filled with a deep, guttural roar. The walls tremble, and the iron chain swings wildly, clanking against the stone. The whispers grow louder, more frantic, filling the air with a cacophony of voices.

From the shadows, a dark shape emerges — a

massive, amorphous figure, its edges flickering like flames, its eyes glowing with a malevolent, fiery light. It moves toward them slowly, deliberately, the darkness seeming to stretch and reach toward them like tendrils.

"It's the darkness!" Eddie shouts, backing away. "It knows we're here!"

Derek grabs Claire's arm, pulling her back. "We need to do something, fast!"

Claire looks down at the journal, then back up at the altar. "We need to light a fire... a pure fire... one that can burn even in this cursed place."

Rachel pulls out a small box of matches from her pocket, her hands shaking. "I... I have these, but... they might not be enough."

Derek takes the matches, his face set with determination. "We have to try. Gather what you can find — anything that will burn."

They scramble around the chamber, finding scraps of fabric, old dried leaves, and pieces of wood.

Derek strikes a match, but it flickers weakly in the cold, damp air. He lights a small pile of leaves, but the fire sputters, struggling to stay alive.

The dark figure moves closer, its roar filling the chamber, and the walls seem to close in on them. The iron chain clatters louder, and the whispers become a deafening scream.

Claire stands over the altar, clutching the journal. "Jonathan said the fire must come from the heart of the mountain... we need to call upon the fire within!"

Rachel looks at her, eyes wide. "But how? How do we summon something like that?"

Eddie's eyes widen, realization dawning on him. "The symbols... they're a spell. We need to chant them... together."

They gather around the altar, their voices trembling as they begin to chant the strange words carved into the stone. The air grows thick with energy, and the symbols on the walls begin to glow brighter, pulsing with a fierce, inner light.

The ground shakes beneath them, and they feel a rush of heat, intense and powerful, rising up from deep within the earth. The fire catches, burning brighter, hotter, until it becomes a blazing inferno, consuming the altar and Annie's remains.

The dark figure lets out a deafening howl, recoiling from the flames, its form dissolving into smoke and shadow. The whispers turn into wails of pain and fury, and then, suddenly, they fall silent.

The fire burns fiercely, and they step back, shielding their faces from the heat. The darkness around them begins to recede, the chamber filling with a warm, golden light.

Claire looks up, tears in her eyes. "We did it... we freed her..."

Rachel nods, her face lit by the flames. "But at what cost?"

As the fire consumes the last of Annie's remains, a

soft, peaceful sigh fills the air, and they feel a warmth spreading through the chamber. The oppressive weight lifts, and for the first time, they feel a sense of calm.

But as they turn to leave, they hear a faint whisper

— a familiar voice, soft and sorrowful: "*Thank you... but beware...*"

The warmth that had filled the chamber suddenly dissipates, replaced by an unsettling chill. They freeze in place, exchanging anxious glances.

Claire's breath catches in her throat as she whispers, "That was Annie... wasn't it?"

Eddie nods, his eyes scanning the dark corners of the chamber. "It sounded like her. But... what does she mean? 'Beware of what?'"

The ground beneath them rumbles again, this time more violently. Loose stones tumble from the ceiling, and the walls seem to pulse with a malevolent energy. The flames on the altar flicker wildly, threatening to be snuffed out by an unseen force.

Derek grabs Rachel's hand, his face set with determination. "We need to get out of here. Now. The mountain... it's waking up."

Rachel tightens her grip on his hand. "She said the fire had to be from the mountain's heart. We summoned it, but... I think we've also awakened something else."

Claire looks back at the altar, where the last embers of the fire still glow faintly. "Jonathan's

curse... the darkness wasn't just about Annie. It was... it was something deeper. Something alive in the mountain itself."

They begin to move toward the cave's entrance, their footsteps quick and frantic, but the cave seems to resist them, shifting and twisting. The path they came down is now narrow and unfamiliar, the walls closing in like a mouth about to swallow them whole. The air grows colder, and the darkness seems to thicken, becoming almost tangible, pressing against their skin.

"Stay close," Derek says, pulling them into a tighter group. "Don't lose sight of each other. This place... it's trying to confuse us."

They press on, but every step feels heavier, like they're wading through thick mud. The whispers return, louder now, filled with anger and anguish, echoing off the walls in an incomprehensible cacophony. Shadows dance in the periphery of their vision, shifting and morphing, as if alive.

Suddenly, Eddie stops and points to a glimmer of light in the distance. "There! That's the way out!"

They push forward with renewed hope, but as they approach, the light flickers and fades, replaced by a solid wall of stone. Eddie curses under his breath. "Damn it! It's playing tricks on us."

Claire takes a deep breath, trying to steady her racing heart. "We need to remember the path we took... focus on the way we came in. The mountain is trying to mislead us... but if we stick

together, we can find the way out."

They close their eyes, trying to picture the cave as they first entered it, visualizing the steps they took, the turns they made. Slowly, they start moving again, step by step, feeling their way through the darkness. The whispers grow louder, almost deafening, but they press on, fighting the fear that grips their hearts.

After what feels like an eternity, they reach a familiar bend in the cave. The air is slightly warmer here, and they hear the faint trickle of water nearby. "This way," Derek urges, pulling them toward the sound.

They hurry forward, their flashlights bobbing in the darkness, and finally, they see it — the faint outline of the cave entrance, the moonlight streaming through the gaps in the vines. Relief floods through them, and they quicken their pace, scrambling toward the exit.

As they burst out of the cave and into the open air, they collapse onto the ground, gasping for breath. The fog has lifted slightly, and they can see the churchyard in the distance, bathed in an eerie silver light.

Rachel looks back at the cave, her face pale. "We made it... but I don't think this is over."

Derek nods, his expression grim. "We may have freed Annie... but whatever was beneath the mountain, whatever darkness Jonathan tried to control... it's still there."

Claire stands, clutching the journal tightly to her chest. "We need to warn the others. The curse may be broken for Annie, but something else... something darker is still out there."

Eddie scans the surrounding woods, his flashlight beam sweeping across the trees. "We need to get out of here, and fast. I don't want to find out what else is lurking in these woods."

They begin to make their way back toward the church, their nerves on edge, every sound magnified in the quiet night. The trees seem to whisper as they pass, their branches swaying in a phantom wind. The fog thickens again, creeping in around their ankles like a living thing.

As they reach the churchyard, they see a figure standing in the doorway — a woman, her form illuminated by the faint glow of the moon. She raises a hand, waving them over. "Claire! Derek! Rachel! Eddie!"

It's Annie. But something about her seems... different. Her face is softer, more peaceful, but her eyes are still shadowed with a sadness that seems to stretch across time.

"You did it," she says, her voice filled with gratitude. "You broke the curse... freed me from my torment. But you must leave now. The mountain... it is awake, and it will not rest."

Rachel steps forward, her heart pounding in her chest. "Annie, what do we do? How do we stop it?"

Annie shakes her head slowly. "You cannot stop it. You can only escape it. The darkness will always be drawn to this place... to those who seek its power. Leave while you can... warn others to stay away."

Claire reaches out, tears in her eyes. "We're sorry, Annie... for everything."

Annie smiles, a sad, knowing smile. "I know. But it is not your burden to bear. Go... and remember... sometimes the only way to defeat darkness is to turn away from it."

With that, Annie begins to fade, her form dissolving into the mist. The fog rolls in thicker now, swallowing the church, the graveyard, the mountain beyond. The wind picks up, howling through the trees like a mournful wail.

Derek grabs Rachel's hand, pulling her away. "Come on... we need to go. Now."

They turn and run, their feet pounding against the wet earth, the fog closing in around them like a shroud. Behind them, they hear the mountain rumble, a low, deep growl that seems to come from the very core of the earth.

As they make their way down the winding path, the fog thins, and they see the lights of the town below, distant but welcoming. Their breath comes in ragged gasps, their hearts pounding in their chests.

When they finally reach the edge of the woods, they stop and turn back, looking up at Black

Mountain. The fog still clings to its slopes, swirling like a living thing, but the rumbling has stopped. For now.

Rachel looks at the others, her face pale but determined. "We need to tell our story... warn everyone. No one else should ever go up there again."

Derek nods, squeezing her hand. "Agreed. But somehow... I feel like this isn't the end."

Claire glances back at the mountain one last time, the shadows deep and impenetrable. "It never is," she whispers. "Not with something like this..."

They turn and walk away, leaving the mountain and its secrets behind. The fog closes in again, hiding the path they took, and in the distance, they hear a faint whisper carried on the wind:

"Beware..."

They walk faster, not daring to look back.

Chapter 9: "The Descent into Madness"

The four of them return to town, the cold wind biting at their skin, but the fog continues to follow, curling around their ankles like spectral hands trying to drag them back. They rush down the winding road toward the nearest diner, the only place in town still open this late at night. They

burst through the doors, gasping for breath, their faces pale and strained with terror.

Inside, the fluorescent lights are harsh and glaring. The smell of stale coffee and fried food fills the air. A few locals look up from their booths, their faces reflecting curiosity and mild annoyance. The waitress, a middle-aged woman with tired eyes, frowns at them from behind the counter.

"You kids alright?" she asks, her voice thick with suspicion.

Derek, still panting, waves a hand dismissively. "We're... we're fine. Just... just need a moment."

They collapse into a booth near the back, the vinyl seats squeaking under their weight. Rachel is trembling, her eyes darting around as if expecting to see something lurking in the corners of the diner. Eddie reaches for her hand, trying to steady her, but his own hands are shaking.

Claire pulls out Jonathan's journal, her fingers tracing the embossed leather cover. "We need to figure this out... What exactly did we awaken back there?"

Eddie leans in, his voice barely above a whisper. "I don't know, but whatever it is, it isn't happy we're still alive. That mountain... it's like it has a mind of its own now."

Derek nods. "Annie warned us, but I think there's more to this than we realize. That whisper... it wasn't just her. It felt like... like something else was there."

Rachel looks down at the journal, her face drawn and pale. "Do you think there's something in there? Something that can help us understand what we're dealing with?"

Claire flips open the journal, her eyes scanning the pages. The handwriting is shaky, almost frantic in places, as if Jonathan's mind was unraveling the deeper he got into his obsession. She reads aloud:

"*August 12th... The visions are stronger. They whisper in my dreams, calling me to the mountain... A voice not my own. Annie's face appears, but it's twisted, contorted with something I cannot comprehend... It wants more than freedom... It wants...*"

She pauses, feeling a cold shiver run down her spine. "What does it want, Jonathan?" she whispers to herself, turning the page.

Eddie scoffs, trying to shake off the fear gnawing at his insides. "So, what? He went nuts, right? The guy lost his mind up there... Maybe we're just imagining things."

Derek shakes his head, his eyes serious. "No, Eddie... you saw what happened back there. The mountain... it's alive in some way. And it's angry."

The waitress comes over with a pot of coffee, her eyes narrowing at the intensity of their conversation. "You folks sure you're alright?" she asks again, her voice softer this time.

Rachel nods quickly, trying to compose herself. "Just... tired. We've had a long night."

The waitress nods, pouring coffee into their mugs. "Well, you be careful out there. The fog's getting thicker, and these roads ain't safe after dark."

As she walks away, Eddie mutters, "Ain't that the understatement of the year..."

They sit in silence for a few moments, each lost in their own thoughts, the diner's ambient noise filling the air — the clatter of dishes, the hum of the air conditioner, the faint buzz of the overhead lights. The tension is palpable, like a coiled spring ready to snap.

Finally, Claire breaks the silence. "We need to go back," she says quietly.

Rachel's head snaps up, her eyes wide with fear. "Go back? Are you crazy? We barely made it out alive!"

Claire meets her gaze, her expression resolute. "I know, but... there's something in that cave we missed. Something that can help us understand this curse. We need answers, and I think they're still up there, buried in that mountain."

Derek nods slowly. "She's right. We can't just leave this alone. Not after what we've seen."

Eddie groans, rubbing his temples. "You guys are nuts. We barely escaped with our lives, and now you want to go back?"

Claire slams the journal down on the table, her voice rising. "Do you want to spend the rest of your life looking over your shoulder? Feeling like something is following you? Because I don't."

Eddie falls silent, his face conflicted. After a long pause, he finally nods. "Alright, fine. But we go prepared this time. No more surprises."

Rachel sighs, her face pale. "If we're really doing this… we need to plan. We need to know exactly what we're up against."

The door of the diner opens suddenly, letting in a cold gust of wind. A man in a worn leather jacket steps inside, his face hidden under the brim of a cowboy hat. He pauses in the doorway, surveying the room with a sharp gaze. When his eyes land on the group, he narrows them and heads straight for their table.

The man stops in front of them, his presence imposing. He pulls up a chair and sits down without asking, his movements slow and deliberate. "I hear you've been up the mountain," he says, his voice low and gravelly.

Derek glances at the others, then back at the man. "Yeah… we have. Who wants to know?"

The man removes his hat, revealing a weathered face, deeply lined with age and experience. "Name's Roy. Roy Sanders. Been living around here for fifty years. I know more about that mountain than anyone alive… or dead."

Claire leans forward, intrigued. "You know about Annie?"

Roy nods. "Annie, the curse, the things that crawl out of that fog at night… I know it all. And I know you kids stirred something up that shouldn't have

been touched."

Rachel swallows hard. "We didn't mean to. We were just trying to help her…"

Roy lets out a bitter chuckle. "Help her? Ain't nobody helped Annie in a hundred years, and it's not about to start now. That curse is older than her… older than this town. It's in the very bones of the mountain. And now… it's awake."

Eddie frowns. "So, what do we do?"

Roy's eyes darken, his expression grave. "You run. You get as far away from that mountain as you can. And you don't look back."

Claire shakes her head, her resolve firm. "We can't. We need answers. We need to know what we're dealing with."

Roy sighs, his shoulders sagging as if the weight of the world is pressing down on him. "Then you're fools. But if you're set on this... there's something you need to know."

He reaches into his jacket pocket and pulls out an old, yellowed map. He unfolds it carefully, laying it on the table. The map is covered in faded lines and strange symbols, with the outline of Black Mountain looming at the center.

"This here," he points to a spot marked with a small, blood-red X, "is where you need to go. It's an old mineshaft, long abandoned... but there's something down there. Something the miners found back in the 1800s... something they tried to bury and forget."

Claire studies the map, her brow furrowed. "What did they find?"

Roy's face darkens. "I don't know for sure. All I know is they never came back up. And those that did... weren't the same."

Derek leans closer, his voice tense. "How do you know all this?"

Roy's eyes flicker with something like fear. "Because I've seen it... I've seen what that mountain can do. And I lost someone up there once... someone I loved."

Rachel's voice is soft, sympathetic. "Who did you lose?"

Roy's face hardens, his eyes turning cold. "My wife... Annie."

A stunned silence falls over the group as his words sink in. Claire feels a chill run down her spine. "Your wife was...?"

Roy nods. "Headless Annie, they call her now. But she was Annie Sanders... and she was mine."

Eddie leans back, his face pale. "Holy... you're her husband? How is that even possible?"

Roy sighs heavily. "She was taken from me a long time ago, by whatever evil lives in that mountain. And now, it wants more... it's always wanted more."

Claire swallows hard. "Then we need to stop it. For Annie. For everyone."

Roy's eyes flicker with a brief moment of hope. "Maybe... maybe you can. But be warned... if you go back up there, you might not come back down."

Derek stands, his face set with determination. "We've made it this far. We're not turning back now."

Roy nods, a small, sad smile on his lips. "Then may God have mercy on your souls. You're gonna need it."

They gather their things, adrenaline pumping through their veins. As they step outside, the fog has thickened once more, swirling around the streetlights like ghostly hands reaching for the sky. The cold wind bites at their skin, and in the distance, they hear a faint, mournful wail echoing down from the mountain.

Claire pauses at the sound, her heart hammering in her chest. It's a sound she's heard before — a distant, sorrowful wail that seems to come from the depths of the earth itself. She turns to the others, her face pale but resolute.

"We need to get going," she says, her voice steady despite the fear gnawing at her insides. "If Roy is right, that old mineshaft might hold the answers we need."

The group nods, each one feeling the weight of the moment pressing down on them. They head toward Derek's car, their footsteps echoing on the empty street. The fog is so thick now that they can barely see a few feet in front of them.

Derek gets behind the wheel, his knuckles white as he grips the steering wheel. Rachel slides into the seat beside him, her hands trembling. Eddie and Claire climb into the back, the tension between them palpable. The engine roars to life, and Derek pulls out onto the road, the headlights cutting through the dense fog like knives.

For a few moments, they drive in silence, the only sound the hum of the engine and the crunch of gravel under the tires. But then, as they make their way up the mountain road, the air grows colder, and the fog thickens, swirling around them like a living thing.

Rachel shivers, rubbing her arms to ward off the chill. "It feels... different this time," she whispers. "Colder."

Eddie leans forward, peering through the windshield. "It's not just the fog. Look, there's frost on the trees... in August."

Claire narrows her eyes, trying to make sense of the unnatural cold. "It's the mountain," she says. "It's alive... reacting to us. It knows we're coming back."

Derek nods, his face tense. "Then we better be ready for whatever it throws at us."

As they ascend the winding road, the headlights flicker, and the radio cuts out, filling the car with a low, static hum. Derek bangs on the dashboard, cursing under his breath. "Not now... damn it, not now."

The fog thickens even more, almost suffocating in its density. Derek slows the car to a crawl, his eyes narrowed in concentration. The road seems to stretch endlessly before them, a dark and twisted path shrouded in mist.

Claire flips through Jonathan's journal, searching for any clue that might help them. Her fingers tremble as she reads his final entry, the words scrawled in a frantic, uneven hand.

"August 15th... The fog is thicker now, like a living thing. It whispers to me... calls to me. I hear Annie's voice, but it's not her... it's something else. Something darker. I feel it in my bones... a presence, a hunger that grows stronger with every step I take toward the mountain."

She looks up, her face pale. "He knew... he felt it too. This presence, this... hunger."

Rachel's eyes widen, fear creeping into her voice. "A hunger? For what?"

Eddie mutters, "For us, maybe. For our souls, our sanity... who knows?"

Suddenly, a shadow darts across the road, just beyond the reach of the headlights. Derek slams on the brakes, the car skidding to a halt. They all lean forward, squinting into the fog, trying to see what it was.

"What was that?" Claire asks, her voice barely a whisper.

Derek shakes his head, his eyes scanning the road. "I don't know... but it was moving fast."

Eddie reaches into his backpack, pulling out a flashlight. "I'll check it out," he says, his voice steady, though his hands are shaking.

He steps out of the car, the flashlight beam cutting through the fog. The air is colder now, biting at his skin like icy needles. He takes a few cautious steps forward, his breath coming out in puffs of steam.

The others watch, their hearts pounding. The fog seems to close in around Eddie, swallowing him up. For a moment, they can't see him at all, just the faint glow of the flashlight in the mist.

Then, they hear it — a low, guttural growl, echoing through the fog. Eddie stops, his heart racing. "Guys?" he calls back over his shoulder, his voice tight with fear.

Derek and Claire leap out of the car, rushing to his side. "What is it?" Claire asks, her eyes darting around, searching for the source of the sound.

Eddie turns, his face pale. "I don't know... but it's close."

Suddenly, a figure bursts out of the fog, charging toward them. It's moving fast, too fast, its limbs contorted in unnatural angles, its face twisted in a mask of rage. They can't make out the features, but they see enough — the dark, hollow sockets where its eyes should be, the gaping maw that seems to scream silently.

Derek raises his flashlight, shining it directly at the figure. It stops, hesitating in the light, its form flickering like a glitch in reality. Claire grabs

Eddie's arm, pulling him back toward the car. "Get in!" she yells.

They scramble back into the car, slamming the doors shut just as the figure lunges at them. It slams against the side of the car with a sickening thud, its hands clawing at the windows, leaving streaks of frost wherever it touches.

Rachel screams, her voice raw with terror. Derek floors the gas, and the car lurches forward, the tires screeching on the icy road. The figure chases after them, moving impossibly fast, its movements jerky and erratic, like a puppet on tangled strings.

"Go, go, go!" Eddie shouts, his eyes wide with fear.

Derek drives faster, the car bouncing over the uneven road, the fog blurring everything around them. The figure keeps pace, its twisted form illuminated in the rearview mirror. It's gaining on them, its mouth open in a silent scream.

Claire grabs Jonathan's journal, flipping to a page filled with strange symbols and runes. "There has to be something... some way to stop it!" she mutters frantically.

The figure reaches the back of the car, its hand slamming against the rear window. The glass cracks, a web of fractures spreading across the surface. Rachel sobs, clutching her seat, her eyes wide with terror.

"Claire, hurry!" Derek yells, his foot pressing harder on the gas.

Claire's eyes dart over the symbols, trying to find something — anything. She spots a line of text in Jonathan's shaky handwriting: *"Speak these words and bind the shadow to the earth..."*

She begins to chant, her voice low and urgent, the words foreign and harsh on her tongue. The figure pauses, its movements slowing, its form flickering in the mist. The air grows colder, the fog swirling violently around them.

The figure lets out a deafening shriek, its body contorting, limbs flailing wildly. The car shakes, the windows rattling, but Claire keeps chanting, her voice growing stronger.

Suddenly, the figure collapses into itself, vanishing into the fog with a final, haunting wail. The air grows still, the fog thinning slightly, and the car skids to a halt, the engine sputtering.

They sit in stunned silence, their breaths heavy, their hearts racing. Claire lowers the journal, her hands trembling.

Derek turns to her, his face pale. "What... what just happened?"

Claire swallows, her voice shaky. "I don't know... but I think we just... banished it? At least for now."

Rachel lets out a shaky breath, wiping tears from her cheeks. "Can we please not do that again?"

Eddie nods, still gripping the edge of his seat. "Yeah... let's not make a habit of it."

Derek starts the car again, his hands shaking. "Let's get to that mineshaft and find what we need. The sooner we're off this mountain, the better."

As they continue their journey, the fog seems to retreat, but they know it's only a matter of time before the mountain sends something else after them. And they have no idea what lies in wait at the abandoned mineshaft, or if they'll ever make it back out alive.

CHAPTER 10: THE DESCENT INTO DARKNESS

The old mine shaft loomed before them, its entrance like a gaping mouth carved into the side of the mountain. The wooden beams that framed it were rotting, sagging under the weight of decades of neglect. Rusted metal tracks led into the darkness, disappearing into the void beyond. A bitter wind blew from within, carrying the faint, almost imperceptible sound of distant whispers.

Derek stopped the car and killed the engine, the headlights dimming to a soft glow that barely illuminated the entrance. He turned to the others, his face tense and drawn. "This is it," he said quietly. "We either find answers in there or... we don't."

Rachel shivered, staring at the mineshaft. Her fingers tapped nervously on her thigh, a steady rhythm that betrayed her fear. "I've read about this place in the old papers," she murmured. "They called it 'The Pit of Despair.' They said it was cursed, even before Annie."

Eddie, who had been quiet for most of the ride, finally spoke up. "So... what do we know about this place?" His voice was rough, a forced steadiness masking the dread clawing at his insides. "Why would Jonathan come here? What's so special about this mine?"

Claire flipped through Jonathan's journal once more, her fingers grazing over his final notes, scrawled in hurried, panicked handwriting. "He wrote that this was where Annie died... or at least, where she was last seen alive. The miners... they found her body near the entrance, decapitated. No one knows who or what did it."

Derek's jaw tightened. "So, this is where it all started?"

"Yeah," Claire nodded. "And he thought that if he could find something... some clue in here, it might help break the curse. He believed there was something buried with her. Something that tied her spirit to the mountain."

The air grew colder as they spoke, a chill that seeped into their bones. The fog had retreated to the edges of the trees, as if afraid to enter the mineshaft's domain. The mountain seemed to hold its breath, waiting.

"We don't have much time," Derek said, his voice firm. "Let's grab what we need and go in."

They gathered their supplies — flashlights, ropes, a first aid kit, and a bundle of sage that Rachel had insisted on bringing. She had said it was for

"protection," though no one seemed entirely convinced it would help against whatever haunted the depths of the mine.

Eddie hesitated at the entrance, his face a mask of conflicting emotions. "I don't like this," he muttered, his voice barely audible. "I really don't like this."

Claire touched his arm gently. "None of us do. But we have to try. For Jonathan. And for ourselves.

We need to end this."

Eddie nodded, taking a deep breath. "Okay. Let's do it."

They turned on their flashlights, the beams cutting through the thick darkness like fragile swords of light. Slowly, they stepped inside, the sound of their footsteps echoing against the walls. The air was thick and stale, smelling of earth and decay.

Derek led the way, his flashlight steady, his eyes scanning every shadow, every nook and cranny. The tunnel seemed to stretch on forever, a narrow passageway that grew colder with every step. The walls were damp, slick with moisture, and the ground beneath their feet was uneven, littered with rocks and debris.

Rachel followed closely behind, clutching the sage tightly in one hand and her flashlight in the other. She whispered a silent prayer under her breath, her heart pounding in her chest. She had never been particularly religious, but in that moment, she was willing to try anything for protection.

Eddie and Claire brought up the rear, their eyes darting nervously from side to side. Every sound, every creak of wood or drip of water, made them jump. The darkness seemed to press in on them, as if it were alive, a living entity that wanted to swallow them whole.

Suddenly, a low moan echoed through the tunnel, sending a shiver down their spines. They stopped, frozen in place, their flashlights flickering.

"What was that?" Rachel whispered, her voice trembling.

Derek held up a hand for silence, his head tilted to listen. The moan grew louder, closer, a sound filled with pain and despair. It seemed to come from all around them, echoing off the walls.

"It's... it's her," Claire said, her voice barely a whisper. "It's Annie. She's close."

Rachel squeezed her eyes shut, clutching the sage tighter. "We need to keep moving," she urged. "We can't stay here."

Derek nodded and started forward again, more cautiously this time. The tunnel seemed to narrow as they went, the ceiling lowering until they had to stoop to pass through. The air grew colder still, their breath fogging in front of their faces.

Eddie shivered, rubbing his arms. "It's freezing... how is it this cold?"

Claire glanced at him. "It's not natural," she said softly. "It's her... it's Annie. She doesn't want us here."

They pressed on, the darkness growing thicker, the cold more biting. Their flashlights flickered again, and then — without warning — they went out, plunging them into complete darkness.

Rachel let out a small gasp, fumbling with her flashlight. "No, no, no... not now!"

Derek cursed under his breath, shaking his flashlight, but it remained stubbornly dark. "Damn it... everyone, stay close. Don't move."

Claire's heart pounded in her chest. She could hear the others breathing, the sound of their rapid, shallow breaths in the darkness. Then, suddenly, she heard something else — a faint whisper, like a voice carried on the wind.

"Annie," the voice whispered. "Annie..."

Claire swallowed hard, her skin prickling with fear. "Did you hear that?" she asked, her voice barely more than a breath.

"I heard it," Eddie replied, his voice tense. "I don't like it."

The whisper grew louder, closer, as if the source was moving toward them. Claire felt a cold draft against her face, and she shivered, fear clawing at her insides.

"We need to get the lights back on," Derek muttered, his hands trembling as he tried to twist the flashlight's battery compartment open. "Everyone, try your lights again!"

One by one, they flicked their flashlights back on, and, miraculously, the beams cut through the darkness again. The relief was palpable, but short- lived. The tunnel ahead of them had changed.

Where there had been a single, narrow path, there were now two diverging tunnels.

Derek stared at the branching paths, his brow furrowed. "That... that wasn't there before."

"It's the mountain," Rachel whispered. "It's trying to confuse us."

Eddie looked at the two tunnels, his face pale. "Which way do we go?"

Claire closed her eyes, taking a deep breath. She tried to think, to remember something from Jonathan's journal, anything that might help them choose the right path. Then, she remembered a phrase he had written: *Follow the sound of the wind; it carries the truth.*

She opened her eyes and turned to the others. "We need to listen," she said. "For the wind. Jonathan said it would guide us."

They stood in silence, straining to hear over the sound of their own breathing. Then, faintly, they heard it — a soft breeze, barely perceptible, coming from the left tunnel.

Derek nodded. "Left it is, then."

They moved down the left tunnel, the sound of the wind growing louder with every step. It was a strange sound, almost melodic, like a mournful song sung by unseen voices. The walls seemed to close in around them, the air growing colder still.

Rachel clutched the sage tighter, her knuckles white. She whispered softly, her voice barely audible. "Please, please protect us..."

The wind picked up, swirling around them, and with it came the faint sound of laughter — a high, childlike giggle that echoed through the tunnel.

Claire's heart stopped. "Did you hear that?" Eddie nodded, his face pale. "Yeah... I heard it."

The laughter grew louder, closer, until it seemed to surround them. They spun around, their flashlights darting through the darkness, but there was nothing there. Just the empty tunnel, stretching on into the blackness.

"Keep moving," Derek urged. "Don't stop."

They continued forward, the laughter fading into the distance. The tunnel began to widen, opening into a large chamber. In the center of the chamber was an old, rusted mining cart, tipped on its side. The ground was littered with broken tools, chunks of coal, and shards of wood.

Derek stepped forward, his flashlight sweeping across the chamber. "Looks like this was some kind of work area," he muttered.

Rachel moved closer, her eyes scanning the debris. She noticed something in the corner, partially buried under a pile of rocks. "Wait... what's that?"

Eddie shone his flashlight where she pointed, revealing a small, weathered notebook. Claire's heart leapt in her chest. "Jonathan's journal!" she exclaimed, rushing forward to grab it.

But as she reached for it, the wind picked up again, a howling gale that swept through the chamber.

The air grew frigid, and the lights flickered once more. A deep, guttural voice boomed through the chamber, reverberating off the stone walls: "LEAVE THIS PLACE."

The sound was inhuman, low and guttural, like the growl of a beast but layered with something else

— something ancient and wrathful. The force of the voice seemed to shake the very ground beneath their feet, sending vibrations up through their bodies.

Rachel stumbled backward, nearly dropping the sage. "Oh my God," she whispered, eyes wide with terror. "What was that?"

Derek grabbed her arm, steadying her. "Stay close," he urged, his voice tight with urgency. "Don't let go of each other."

Claire, still focused on the notebook, managed to grab it and pull it free from the rocks. She flipped it open, desperate to find some clue, some answer to what was happening. The pages were yellowed and brittle, but she could still make out Jonathan's frantic scrawl:

"She won't let go. She's bound to this place, to this darkness. There's something deeper, something hidden. If you're reading this, I'm sorry... I'm so sorry. I couldn't break the curse. I couldn't save us."

Claire's heart sank. "He didn't find a way to stop

her," she murmured, a cold dread creeping over her. "He was just... lost in here like us."

Eddie's eyes darted around the chamber. "So what do we do now?" he asked, his voice tight with fear. "How do we get out?"

The chamber grew darker, the shadows deepening around them, as if the walls themselves were closing in. The air grew heavy with a thick, acrid smell — a mix of sulfur and decay. The howling wind died down, replaced by a low, rhythmic thumping, like the sound of a distant heartbeat echoing through the stone.

Rachel looked around wildly, clutching the sage in front of her like a talisman. "We need to move. We can't stay here. This place... it's alive."

Derek nodded, his face grim. "Back the way we came," he decided. "We're not getting answers here, just more danger."

But as they turned to leave, the tunnel behind them was gone — replaced by a solid wall of rock.

Derek's eyes widened. "What the hell...? No, no, no, this wasn't here before!"

Panic surged through them. The path was sealed, the only exit vanished. Claire's breath came in short, panicked gasps. "It's trapping us," she realized. "It doesn't want us to leave."

Eddie swore under his breath, kicking at the wall in frustration. "We're stuck. We're completely trapped!"

Rachel's eyes darted to the notebook in Claire's

hands. "What else does it say?" she asked desperately. "Is there anything, any clue?"

Claire flipped through the pages, her hands shaking. The writing grew more chaotic, Jonathan's thoughts more fragmented. Then she found a page with a crude drawing —

a symbol, etched with jagged lines, surrounded by scribbled words: *"The seal... break the seal to break the curse."*

"There!" she exclaimed, showing the page to the others. "There's a seal... some kind of symbol. If we can find it, maybe we can get out of here."

Derek studied the drawing. "Okay, but where do we start looking? This place could be miles deep."

A faint scratching noise interrupted him, coming from the far side of the chamber. It was slow, deliberate, like nails scraping against stone. They turned their flashlights in unison, the beams landing on the far wall where, slowly, an outline began to appear — a figure etched into the stone, its form twisting and moving as if alive.

The figure grew clearer, its details emerging from the darkness. It was a woman, her face hidden in shadow, but her body contorted, her arms outstretched in a grotesque, unnatural pose. And then, in the center of her chest, they saw it — the same symbol from Jonathan's drawing, glowing faintly, pulsing like a heartbeat.

"That's it," Claire whispered, her voice trembling. "That's the seal."

But before anyone could move, the figure began to shift, the stone cracking and crumbling around it. The figure's arms began to reach outward, the stone turning to flesh, the fingers curling into claws. The face slowly emerged from the shadow, revealing a hollow, gaping void where a head should be.

Rachel let out a scream, dropping the sage. "It's her! Oh God, it's her!"

Derek grabbed a rock from the ground, his face set with determination. "We have to destroy the seal," he shouted. "Now!"

But as he lunged toward the figure, the ground beneath them shook violently, and the walls began to close in, as if the entire chamber was alive and angry. The heartbeat grew louder, pounding in their ears, drowning out all other sounds.

Eddie and Claire grabbed Derek, pulling him back just as a chunk of rock fell from the ceiling, narrowly missing him. "We can't just rush at it!" Eddie yelled. "There's got to be another way!"

Rachel picked up the sage again, frantically trying to light it with a trembling hand. "We need to weaken her hold," she said, her voice breaking. "Sage is supposed to cleanse evil spirits... maybe it can buy us time!"

Derek nodded, catching his breath. "Do it," he urged. "Anything to slow her down."

Rachel managed to get the sage lit, and as it began to burn, she waved it toward the figure. The smoke curled through the air, reaching out like tendrils. For a moment, the figure seemed to hesitate, the glow in its chest dimming slightly.

"It's working!" Claire shouted. "Keep going, Rachel!"

Rachel continued waving the sage, her voice growing stronger as she recited a prayer she barely remembered from childhood. The air seemed to shift, the heartbeat slowing, the stone walls trembling less violently.

But then, the figure's hands burst into flame, and the stone began to melt away, revealing flesh underneath. The symbol on its chest flared bright again, and it stepped forward, its headless form moving with a terrible, unnatural grace.

"It's not enough," Derek muttered, fear in his eyes. "We need to destroy that symbol, or it's going to kill us all!"

Eddie looked around, spotting a rusted metal rod among the debris. He grabbed it, holding it like a weapon. "Cover me," he said, determination hardening his features. "I'm going for it."

Derek nodded, moving to stand beside Rachel, who was still wielding the sage. "We'll try to keep it distracted. Go!"

With a yell, Eddie charged at the figure, the rod raised high. As he reached it, he swung with all his strength, aiming for the glowing symbol on its chest. The figure raised a clawed hand to block him, but Derek and Rachel lunged forward,

throwing handfuls of burning sage at its feet.

The figure shrieked, a horrible, earsplitting sound that seemed to pierce through their very souls.

Eddie swung again, striking the symbol dead center. The glow flickered, then flared bright, blinding them with a burst of white light.

The chamber shook violently, the walls beginning to crack and crumble. The headless figure let out another shriek, more desperate this time, and its body began to dissolve, turning to ash and dust in the wind.

The glow from the symbol faded, the stone beneath it crumbling away. The heartbeat sound slowed, then stopped altogether. The air grew still, the cold receding, the chamber settling into an uneasy silence.

They all stood there, breathing heavily, their hearts racing, unsure if it was truly over.

Rachel finally broke the silence. "Did we... did we do it?"

Derek nodded, his face still pale, but there was a glimmer of hope in his eyes. "I think so," he replied. "At least, for now. We need to get out of here, before the mountain decides to trap us again."

Claire clutched the notebook tightly, a new resolve burning in her eyes. "Jonathan couldn't break the curse, but we found something he didn't. We know more now... we're closer. We have to keep going, find the next clue. We're not leaving until we

finish this."

Eddie nodded, his grip on the metal rod relaxing. "Let's move," he said, a hint of determination in his voice. "Let's find a way out and get ready for whatever comes next."

They turned toward the newly opened tunnel ahead, their flashlights cutting through the darkness. The path was uncertain, the danger far from over, but they had survived one more encounter with the terror that lurked in the shadows of Black Mountain.

And as they moved forward, deeper into the unknown, they knew one thing for sure — they were not alone.

CHAPTER 11: THE CURSED PATH

The cave entrance loomed ahead, a jagged black maw yawning into the depths of the mountain. An oppressive silence hung in the air, pressing against them like a heavy weight. Rachel's flashlight beam flickered over the ancient rock walls, revealing faint carvings — symbols that seemed to twist and move just out of sight. The atmosphere was thick with tension, as if the mountain itself were holding its breath, waiting.

They hesitated at the threshold, unsure whether to continue or to turn back. The sense of dread had only grown stronger since their last encounter with Headless Annie. The air was colder here, and it smelled of damp earth and something else —

something acrid, metallic, like old blood.

"Whatever is in there... it's waiting for us," Eddie muttered, his voice barely a whisper.

Claire clutched the notebook against her chest, her hands trembling. She glanced back at the others, trying to muster some courage. "We have to keep going. We've come this far, and the only way out is forward."

Derek nodded, though his eyes betrayed his fear. "We need to stick together. If something happens, no one goes off alone. Agreed?"

Rachel was the first to respond. "Agreed," she said, though her voice was thin, almost wavering. She had been trying to keep it together for the group's sake, but she could feel the fear clawing at her insides, a primal terror that whispered of doom.

With a deep breath, they stepped inside, their footsteps echoing eerily down the stone passage. The cave walls seemed to close in around them, narrowing as they descended deeper into the mountain. The temperature dropped further, the cold seeping into their bones. Rachel's breath puffed in the air like smoke, her hand tightening around the flashlight.

"Anyone else feel that?" Derek asked, rubbing his arms. "It's like... something's watching us."

"I've felt it since we got here," Rachel replied, trying to sound braver than she felt. "Like there are eyes in the dark... just waiting."

Eddie nodded, his grip tightening on the metal rod he still carried. "If something's out there, we'll be ready. Just keep your eyes open."

They continued down the passage, the air growing heavier with each step. The flickering beams of their flashlights revealed strange markings on the walls — ancient symbols carved deep into the rock, their meanings lost to time. Some looked like runes, others like primitive drawings of faces, twisted and contorted in pain or fear.

Claire's heart pounded in her chest as she stared at the symbols. "What do you think these mean?" she asked, her voice echoing down the tunnel.

"Warnings," Rachel replied grimly. "Maybe even curses. This place... it's like a graveyard for souls."

They rounded a corner, and the tunnel opened up into a vast chamber. A low, mournful wail filled the air, seeming to come from everywhere and nowhere at once. The sound was unearthly, like the cry of a lost soul or a dying animal. It set their nerves on edge, and they paused, listening intently.

"What was that?" Eddie whispered, his eyes wide with fear.

Claire shivered, feeling a chill run down her spine. "It sounds like... like someone crying."

"No," Derek said, shaking his head. "Not someone. Something."

Rachel turned, her flashlight catching something on the far wall of the chamber — a shadow, tall and thin, standing just at the edge of the light. It

didn't move, didn't make a sound, but its presence was undeniable.

"There's something there," she said, pointing. "Look."

They all turned, their flashlights converging on the spot. The shadow didn't vanish; instead, it seemed to grow darker, more solid, until they could make out the faint outline of a figure — a woman, headless, her body clothed in a tattered white dress that seemed to float just above the ground.

"Annie," Claire whispered, feeling the name catch in her throat like a thorn.

The figure moved, slowly at first, then faster, drifting toward them with an unnatural grace. The air around them grew colder, the temperature dropping sharply. The wailing grew louder, more insistent, echoing off the stone walls.

"Run!" Derek shouted, grabbing Claire's arm and pulling her back toward the tunnel. They all turned and bolted, their footsteps pounding against the rock floor. The figure gave chase, gliding effortlessly behind them, closing the distance with terrifying speed.

Rachel glanced back, her breath coming in short gasps. "She's getting closer!" she yelled, panic rising in her voice.

Eddie skidded to a halt, raising the metal rod. "Keep going!" he shouted. "I'll hold her off!"

"No!" Rachel screamed, grabbing his arm. "You can't face her alone!"

Eddie hesitated, his resolve wavering. But before he could decide, the figure was upon them, its cold, spectral hand reaching out. Eddie swung the rod with all his might, but it passed right through her, as if she were made of smoke.

The figure laughed — a hollow, mocking sound that seemed to come from everywhere at once. Eddie stumbled back, his eyes wide with fear. "What... what the hell?"

"She's not real," Claire whispered, realization dawning on her. "She's a projection... a manifestation of the curse!"

Derek grabbed Rachel's hand. "Then let's keep moving! Don't let her touch you!"

They ran, deeper into the tunnel, the laughter following them, growing louder and more distorted. The shadows seemed to move on their own, shifting and twisting, reaching out with long, claw-like fingers.

Rachel's mind raced. "There has to be a way to break the illusion!" she shouted. "Think! What does she want? Why is she doing this?"

"Revenge," Claire replied, her voice tight with fear. "She's angry... she wants someone to suffer like she did."

The tunnel sloped downward, and they stumbled, trying to keep their footing. The air grew even colder, their breath freezing in the air. They could feel the presence of something dark and malevolent, pressing in from all sides.

"She's feeding off our fear," Derek said, his voice strained. "We need to stay calm... stay focused."

But it was easier said than done. The shadows seemed to close in around them, whispering in low, guttural voices. The wailing grew louder, more insistent, as if it were inside their heads.

Rachel felt a surge of panic. "I can't... I can't do this," she whispered, her voice breaking. "It's too much."

Claire grabbed her hand, squeezing it tightly. "Yes, you can," she insisted. "We're in this together.

We've made it this far. Don't give up now."

They pushed forward, stumbling over rocks and debris, their flashlights flickering as the batteries began to die. The shadows grew thicker, darker, until it felt like they were moving through a living, breathing entity.

Derek stopped, holding up a hand. "Wait... listen."

They all stopped, holding their breath. The wailing had stopped, replaced by a low, rhythmic sound — a heartbeat, slow and steady, coming from somewhere deep within the mountain.

"It's her heart," Claire whispered, her eyes wide with realization. "It's the source of her power. We need to find it... destroy it."

"But where?" Eddie asked, looking around frantically. "Where is it?"

Rachel closed her eyes, trying to focus. "Think... think like her," she muttered. "If you were trapped, bound to this place... where would you hide your heart?"

They all fell silent, listening to the heartbeat. It seemed to be coming from everywhere, resonating through the stone, pulsing like a drumbeat in their chests.

Derek took a deep breath. "We split up," he suggested. "Cover more ground. We'll find it faster."

"No!" Rachel objected, panic in her eyes. "We promised to stay together!"

"We don't have a choice!" Derek argued. "She's getting stronger. If we don't find it soon, we're dead!"

Claire nodded, reluctantly agreeing. "Okay, but we stay within shouting distance. If anyone sees anything, call out."

They split up, each taking a different tunnel, their footsteps echoing in the darkness. The heartbeat grew louder, more insistent, like a countdown to their doom.

Rachel felt her way along the tunnel, her flashlight barely illuminating the path ahead. The shadows seemed to shift and move, whispering her name, taunting her. She forced herself to ignore them, focusing on the heartbeat.

Suddenly, she saw it — a faint, pulsing light at the end of the tunnel. Her heart leapt with hope. "I found it!" she shouted, turning to call the others. But as she turned, she saw something that made

her blood run cold.

The figure of Headless Annie was standing right behind her, inches away, its hollow, eyeless face staring directly at her. She froze, unable to move, her breath caught in her throat.

"Rachel!" Claire's voice echoed from somewhere nearby. "Are you okay?"

Rachel couldn't speak, couldn't move. The figure reached out, its hand cold and spectral, and touched her shoulder. The cold was like nothing she had ever felt, seeping deep into her bones, freezing her from the inside out.

"Rachel!" Claire's voice was more urgent now, closer.

Rachel finally found her voice. "Help... me..." she whispered, her voice barely audible.

The figure leaned in closer, its headless form seeming to loom over her, its mouth opening in a silent scream. The chill intensified, piercing through her chest like an icy blade. She felt her legs buckle, her body trembling as fear gripped her heart. The shadows around her seemed to close in, thick and suffocating, like a living shroud.

"Rachel!" Claire's voice was desperate now, echoing down the tunnels, coming closer. "Hold on! I'm coming!"

Rachel's eyes locked onto the empty void where the figure's face should have been, her mind racing with fragments of thought — memories, regrets, and fear all crashing together. She struggled to

remember the warmth of her family, the reason she had come on this trip, the fight for survival that had brought them this far. It felt like her mind was slipping away, pulled into the cold abyss of Annie's presence.

The headless figure began to tilt its form, almost as if it was examining her, contemplating something unspeakable. Then, slowly, it raised its hand again, and Rachel could see the ghostly, translucent fingers, bones visible beneath the mist-like skin.

She felt her body start to weaken, her senses dulling.

But then, just as the figure reached for her once more, there was a sudden shout.

"Rachel, get down!" Derek's voice boomed from behind her.

She didn't think — she dropped to the ground instinctively, and a second later, there was a flash of light. Derek had grabbed a flare from his pack and hurled it directly at the figure. The flare burst into a brilliant, blinding light, the flames licking up with a harsh, red glow. The figure recoiled, hissing like steam hitting water, and the shadows seemed to pull back, melting away from the intense light.

The ghostly form of Headless Annie twisted and writhed in agony, the light from the flare burning through her like acid. The sound of her wail was deafening, a scream that pierced through the air, shaking the walls of the cave itself. Her form flickered, becoming less substantial, her outline blurring and fading as if caught in a strong wind.

Claire rushed to Rachel's side, helping her to her feet. "Rachel, are you okay?" she asked, her voice trembling.

Rachel nodded weakly, her legs shaking. "I... I think so," she stammered, still feeling the cold deep in her bones. "But we have to hurry... we need to find that heart."

Derek stepped forward, the flare still burning brightly in his hand. "Whatever we do, we need to do it fast. This thing is buying us time, but not much."

They turned back toward the faint, pulsing light that Rachel had spotted at the end of the tunnel. Now, with the figure momentarily weakened, the light seemed brighter, more distinct. It had a rhythm, a steady beat that matched the sound echoing through the cave — the heartbeat.

"That's it!" Claire shouted. "The heart! It's in there!"

They rushed toward the light, the tunnel opening up into another chamber. This one was smaller, more intimate, with walls covered in more of the strange symbols and carvings. In the center of the room, on a makeshift stone altar, lay a small object, wrapped in layers of decayed cloth. The light was coming from within, a soft, pulsating glow that seemed to synchronize with the thumping heartbeat they had been following.

Rachel took a step forward, her hand reaching out toward the object, but Derek grabbed her arm.

"Wait," he warned. "It could be a trap."

Claire stepped closer, examining the altar, the symbols. "These markings... they look like some kind of binding spell," she murmured. "An ancient one, probably meant to contain her spirit. But if that's her heart... destroying it should break the curse."

"Then let's not waste any time," Eddie said, stepping forward with determination. He raised his metal rod, ready to strike.

But before he could bring it down, the shadows around them began to move again. The chamber darkened, the air growing colder. The figure of Headless Annie reappeared at the entrance, her form flickering but more solid than before. She let out a blood-curdling scream, the sound reverberating through the cave like an explosion.

"She's trying to stop us!" Derek yelled. "Do it now, Eddie!"

Eddie swung the rod down with all his strength, smashing it into the heart-shaped object on the altar. There was a loud crack, a burst of light, and a shockwave that knocked them all backward. The cave shook, dust and debris falling from the ceiling as the force of the impact seemed to ripple through the mountain itself.

The object on the altar shattered, the light within flaring up one last time before going out completely. The heartbeat stopped, the sound cutting off abruptly, leaving a sudden, profound

silence in its wake.

The figure of Headless Annie let out a final, agonized wail, her form disintegrating into a cloud of mist. For a moment, they could see the outline of a woman's face in the fog, eyes filled with sorrow and pain. Then, with a gust of cold wind, she was gone — the mist dissipating into nothingness, the cave falling silent once more.

They stood there, panting, hearts racing, the weight of what had just happened settling over them like a heavy blanket. The oppressive cold began to lift, replaced by a faint warmth that slowly seeped into their bones.

"Is it... over?" Claire whispered, barely daring to hope.

Rachel nodded slowly. "I think so," she replied, though her voice was still shaky. "I think... we did it."

Eddie dropped the rod, his hands trembling. "Let's get out of here," he said, his voice thick with emotion. "I've had enough of this place."

They turned and began to make their way back through the tunnel, feeling the shadows retreating, the air growing warmer with every step. But even as they left the chamber behind, they couldn't shake the feeling that something had changed — something deep within the mountain, and within themselves.

As they emerged into the night air, the stars overhead shining brightly, they knew that they

would never forget what they had seen — and they could only hope that, this time, Headless Annie would find peace.

CHAPTER 12: THE WHISPERING WOODS

The group stepped out of the cave, breathing in the cold, crisp night air. Their breaths came in short, misty puffs, and for a moment, they stood in silence, listening to the sounds of the mountain.

The weight of what had just happened lingered over them like a thick fog. The stars seemed to blink down from the sky, bright and indifferent, and the dense forest surrounding the cave was alive with sounds: the distant hoot of an owl, the rustle of leaves in the wind, and something else — something low and barely audible, like a faint whisper threading through the trees.

Rachel rubbed her arms, trying to shake off the lingering cold from the cave. "Do you hear that?" she asked, her voice barely above a whisper.

Eddie turned his head, his brow furrowing. "Hear what?"

Claire took a step closer to Rachel, nodding. "The whispering... it's like the trees are talking."

Derek shrugged, though his shoulders were tense. "Probably just the wind," he muttered, but his eyes darted nervously around the forest. The trees seemed to loom over them, their branches twisted and gnarled, like skeletal fingers reaching out to grab them.

They all stood for a moment, straining to hear. The whispering grew slightly louder, just enough to distinguish individual words, though they were jumbled and overlapping, like a chorus of voices speaking all at once. It was impossible to make out what they were saying, but the tone was unmistakable — urgent, warning, almost pleading.

"Okay, that's definitely not the wind," Eddie whispered, gripping his rod tightly. His knuckles were white, his face pale.

Rachel nodded, her heart pounding in her chest. "We need to get off this mountain. Whatever we did back there... it might not be over."

Claire glanced back at the cave entrance, which now seemed like a yawning, black mouth ready to swallow them whole. "We destroyed the heart, right? That should have ended it... but what if—"

"What if we unleashed something else?" Derek finished, his voice low and tense. "Something that was trapped here with Annie."

The whispering seemed to swell in response, growing louder, more insistent. The words were still indistinguishable, but the tone had changed — it was sharper now, more hostile, like a rising tide of anger.

Rachel shivered. "Let's just keep moving. The longer we stay, the worse it's going to get."

They started down the narrow path through the woods, the darkness pressing in around them. Their flashlights cast long, flickering shadows on

the ground, and every step seemed to echo, the sound swallowed by the dense forest. The air felt thick, heavy, charged with an electric tension that made the hairs on the back of their necks stand on end.

As they moved deeper into the forest, the whispering seemed to follow them, surrounding them from all sides. It was as if the very trees were alive, their leaves rustling with unseen mouths.

The forest felt different now — more malevolent, like it was watching them, waiting.

"I don't like this," Claire muttered, her voice tight with fear. "I feel like we're walking into a trap."

Derek nodded. "I think we are," he said grimly. "But there's no turning back now."

Suddenly, Eddie stopped dead in his tracks. "Did you see that?" he whispered, his eyes wide, staring into the darkness.

"See what?" Rachel asked, her grip tightening on her flashlight.

"There!" Eddie pointed toward a cluster of trees. "Something moved... something big."

They all turned to look, their flashlights sweeping through the trees. At first, they saw nothing, just the dark, impenetrable shadows. But then, Rachel saw it — a flicker of movement, something pale and spectral darting between the trees.

"There!" she gasped. "Did you see it?"

Claire nodded, her face pale. "It looked like... a woman, but she was moving too fast."

Derek swallowed hard. "No, not a woman... more like a shadow of one."

The whispering grew louder again, and this time, the voices were filled with malice. The wind picked up, rustling the leaves with a sound like distant laughter, mocking and cruel.

"Keep moving," Derek urged. "Whatever it is, it's trying to scare us."

They pressed on, moving faster now, but the whispering followed them, growing louder, more intense. The forest seemed to close in around them, the trees leaning in like they were trying to listen, their branches creaking and groaning.

Eddie glanced over his shoulder, his face tight with fear. "This isn't right... this isn't normal," he muttered.

"None of this is normal," Claire replied. "We're dealing with forces we don't understand."

Suddenly, the ground beneath them shifted, a deep rumbling sound echoing through the forest. The earth trembled, and they stumbled, barely keeping their footing.

"What the hell was that?" Rachel exclaimed, panic rising in her voice.

"An earthquake?" Eddie suggested, but he didn't sound convinced.

The rumbling stopped, and for a moment, there was a heavy, oppressive silence. Then, from

somewhere deep in the forest, they heard it — a long, low moan, like the sound of something ancient waking up.

Rachel's eyes widened. "That didn't sound like an earthquake."

"No," Derek agreed, his voice barely above a whisper. "That sounded like something alive."

The whispering swelled to a roar, and the trees seemed to bend toward them, their branches reaching out like claws.

The forest floor trembled again, and they heard the sound of something moving through the underbrush — something big, and getting closer.

"Run!" Derek shouted, and they took off, sprinting down the path. The forest seemed to come alive around them, the trees swaying and creaking, the whispering voices growing louder and more frantic. Shadows darted between the trees, and they could hear the sound of footsteps — heavy, thudding footsteps, like something was chasing them.

Rachel's heart pounded in her chest as she ran, her breath coming in short, ragged gasps. She could feel the cold sweat trickling down her back, her muscles burning with effort. She glanced over her shoulder and saw a flash of white — the spectral figure moving through the trees, impossibly fast, closing the distance between them.

"Faster!" she yelled, pushing herself harder. They burst out of the dense forest onto a narrow,

rocky ledge. Below them, the mountain dropped away into darkness, a sheer cliff face that seemed to go on forever. The whispering voices were deafening now, a cacophony of rage and fear.

Derek skidded to a stop, panting. "We can't go any further!" he shouted. "It's a dead end!"

They turned, back to back, facing the forest. The spectral figure was there, hovering just beyond the tree line, its form flickering and shifting in the moonlight. It had no face, just a dark, empty void where its head should have been, and its arms were outstretched, fingers curling like claws.

Claire's voice was shaking. "What do we do now?"

Rachel's mind raced. She could feel the fear clawing at her insides, threatening to overwhelm her, but she forced herself to focus. "We stand our ground," she said, her voice steady. "Whatever this is, we face it together."

The figure stepped closer, the air around them growing colder, and the whispering reached a fever pitch. They could feel the ground trembling beneath their feet, the cliff edge crumbling slightly under the weight of the tension.

Derek pulled out a lighter and a bottle of alcohol from his pack. "This is all I've got left," he muttered. "If we're going down, we're going down fighting."

He flicked the lighter, the small flame dancing in the darkness. "Come on," he whispered, "show us

what you've got."

The figure paused, its form wavering, and for a moment, they thought it might retreat. But then it surged forward with a sudden, violent burst of speed, its arms outstretched, and they knew there was no escaping it.

With a shout, Derek hurled the bottle at the figure, the glass shattering against its form. The alcohol ignited in a brilliant burst of flames, and the figure let out a high-pitched scream, its form dissolving into smoke.

For a moment, they stood there, breathing heavily, the flames casting flickering shadows across their faces. The whispering had stopped, replaced by a deep, eerie silence.

But then, from somewhere deep within the forest, they heard it again — the low, rumbling moan of something ancient and hungry.

And they knew that this was far from over.

CHAPTER 13: THE SHADOW'S GRASP

The silence was suffocating, pressing in on the group as they stood on the narrow ledge, the dying embers of the alcohol fire casting long, jagged shadows on the rocks around them. The moan from deep within the forest seemed to echo across the mountainside, vibrating in their bones like an ominous, low-pitched growl. Each of them felt it in their core — a primal warning, like the roar of a predator in the dark.

Claire clutched her flashlight tightly, her knuckles turning white. Her mind was racing with memories of stories her grandmother used to tell — old Appalachian tales about creatures and spirits that lived in the woods, lurking in the shadows. She'd never truly believed them, always thought they were just stories meant to scare kids into behaving. But now, with every nerve in her body screaming that they were being watched, she couldn't help but feel the weight of those tales like a stone in her stomach.

"Did you hear that?" Eddie asked, his voice a tight whisper, almost swallowed by the stillness around them.

Rachel nodded, fear evident in her eyes. "It's coming from deeper in the forest," she murmured. "Something else... something bigger."

Derek moved closer to the group, his eyes never leaving the dark tree line. "We need to find another way off this ledge," he said firmly, trying to keep his voice steady, even though his heart was hammering in his chest. "We can't stay here. If that... thing comes back, we're sitting ducks."

Rachel's hands were trembling, but she forced herself to focus. She looked over the edge of the cliff, down into the darkness below. The drop was steep, but not insurmountable. "There's a narrow path down there," she pointed out. "It looks like it might lead us around the mountain... maybe to safety."

Eddie nodded. "It's better than staying up here.

But it's going to be risky."

"Everything's a risk at this point," Derek replied. "Let's move."

One by one, they began to make their way down the path, carefully navigating the jagged rocks and loose gravel. The descent was treacherous — each step sending small stones skittering down the slope into the abyss below. The whispering had stopped, but the tension hung thick in the air, as if the forest itself was holding its breath, waiting for something.

As they moved, Claire kept glancing back over her shoulder, half-expecting to see the spectral figure of Headless Annie reappear, its form shifting and flickering in the moonlight. But there was nothing

— just the still, dark forest and the distant glow of the cave mouth, growing fainter as they descended.

After what felt like an eternity, they reached a flat stretch of ground, a narrow plateau that jutted out from the side of the mountain. The forest loomed close around them, the trees casting long, spindly shadows in the moonlight. They paused, catching their breath, each of them acutely aware of how vulnerable they were out here in the open.

"Where to now?" Eddie asked, his voice strained.

Rachel scanned the area, her flashlight sweeping over the trees. "There's a path," she said, pointing toward a narrow trail that wound its way into the thick woods. "It looks like it goes around the mountain… but it's hard to tell."

Derek looked at the path, his brow furrowed. "It's our best shot," he said finally. "We need to keep moving."

They started down the trail, moving as quickly and quietly as they could. The forest closed in around them, the trees crowding close, their branches interwoven like a tangled web. The air grew colder, the temperature dropping with every step, and the faint mist began to rise from the ground, swirling around their ankles like ghostly tendrils.

Rachel felt her heart pounding in her chest, every sense on high alert. She could hear the faint crunch of leaves underfoot, the soft rustle of branches, and somewhere in the distance, the low, rhythmic thumping of the heart she thought they had destroyed.

"Do you hear that?" she whispered to Claire, who was walking beside her.

Claire nodded, her face pale. "It's the heartbeat… it's still there."

"But how?" Rachel asked, a cold shiver running down her spine. "We destroyed it… didn't we?"

Claire's eyes darted nervously to the shadows. "Maybe it wasn't the heart," she replied, her voice trembling. "Maybe… maybe it was something else."

Derek, who had been leading the group, suddenly stopped and held up a hand. "Quiet," he whispered. "Do you hear that?"

They all fell silent, straining to listen. At first,

there was nothing — just the soft rustle of leaves in the wind. But then, they heard it — a faint, rhythmic chanting, like a distant chorus of voices, rising and falling in a slow, hypnotic cadence.

"What is that?" Eddie whispered, his eyes wide with fear.

"It sounds like... singing," Rachel murmured, her heart pounding.

Derek shook his head. "No... not singing," he said, his voice tight. "It's a ritual. A summoning."

Claire felt a chill run down her spine. "A summoning for what?" she asked, though she wasn't sure she wanted to know the answer.

Derek's face was grim. "Something powerful... something ancient. And it's close."

They kept moving, the chanting growing louder with every step. The path twisted and turned, weaving deeper into the forest, the trees growing thicker and darker. The air was heavy with the scent of damp earth and decaying leaves, and the mist was thicker now, swirling around their legs, making it hard to see the ground in front of them.

Rachel's flashlight flickered, and for a moment, she thought she saw movement in the fog — a shadowy figure darting between the trees. She froze, her heart hammering in her chest. "Did you see that?" she whispered to Claire.

Claire nodded, her eyes wide. "Something's following us," she whispered back.

Derek turned, his expression tense. "Keep moving," he urged. "Don't look back."

They picked up the pace, their footsteps crunching loudly on the leaf-covered ground. The chanting was louder now, almost deafening, and the shadows seemed to move around them, darting in and out of the mist like phantoms.

Suddenly, the path opened up into a small clearing, and they stumbled to a stop, their breath coming in short, ragged gasps. In the center of the clearing was a large stone circle, ancient and weathered, covered in strange symbols that seemed to glow faintly in the moonlight. Around the circle stood several hooded figures, their faces hidden in the shadows, their hands raised in supplication.

Rachel's blood ran cold. "What is this?" she whispered, her voice trembling.

Derek's face was pale. "A ritual site," he said, his voice barely audible. "This is where they're calling it from."

CHAPTER 14: THE RITUAL UNLEASHED

The clearing felt like a trap, a space carved out of the forest for something sinister and ancient. The air seemed to vibrate with a deep, low hum, resonating through their bones. The hooded figures around the stone circle moved slowly, rhythmically swaying as they chanted in a language none of them recognized. Their voices were low and gravelly, the words guttural, filled with an eerie

resonance that sent chills down Rachel's spine.

Rachel's hands trembled as she held her flashlight, its beam flickering over the symbols on the stones. They seemed to pulse, as if alive, their shapes shifting and twisting in the dim light. "Those symbols..." she whispered, "I've seen them before."

Claire's eyes darted over the stones, her mind racing. "Where?" she asked, her voice tight with fear.

"In my grandmother's books," Rachel replied. "They were in the section about ancient curses... rituals to summon or bind spirits. This isn't just any ritual... it's powerful. Dangerous."

Derek took a cautious step forward, his eyes never leaving the hooded figures. "We have to stop this," he said, his voice steady but his hands shaking. "Whatever they're calling... it can't be good."

Eddie swallowed hard. "How? There are too many of them, and we don't even know what they're doing."

Derek clenched his jaw. "We don't need to know what they're doing. We just need to break the circle."

Rachel looked at him, eyes wide. "Break the circle? You're talking about interrupting a ritual that's been in the making for God knows how long. What if that makes things worse?"

Derek turned to face her, his face set with determination. "It's a risk we have to take. Do you

want to wait around and find out what they're summoning?"

The chanting grew louder, and the air felt charged with energy, crackling like electricity just before a storm. The mist swirled around their feet, and the ground seemed to tremble beneath them.

Eddie's breath quickened. "Okay, okay," he stammered. "But we have to be smart about this. If we go rushing in, we're dead."

Claire nodded, swallowing her fear. "I agree. We need to distract them... draw them away from the circle. Then we break it."

Derek's eyes lit up with an idea. "The flares," he said. "Eddie, do you still have those flares in your pack?"

Eddie nodded quickly, fumbling with his backpack. "Yeah, yeah... got 'em right here."

Derek grabbed a flare, cracking it open with a hiss. The bright red light illuminated the clearing, causing the hooded figures to falter in their chant, momentarily distracted by the sudden blaze of light. "Throw them around," Derek instructed. "Make them think they're surrounded."

They each grabbed a flare, igniting them and tossing them into the woods around the clearing. The flares landed with a bright, sizzling flash, the red glow casting long shadows across the trees.

The hooded figures hesitated, their heads turning to the source of the light, the chanting faltering into a confused murmur.

Rachel took a deep breath. "Now's our chance," she whispered. "Go!"

They surged forward, hearts pounding, moving as one toward the stone circle. Derek reached the edge first, skidding to a stop in front of one of the stones. Without hesitation, he shoved it with all his strength, trying to topple it over. The stone was heavy, rooted deep into the ground, but it shifted slightly under his weight.

The chanting resumed, louder and more frenzied, and the figures began to move toward them, their hands raised as if to cast something unseen. The air grew colder, and the mist thickened, swirling up from the ground like smoke.

"Hurry!" Claire shouted, fear edging her voice. "They're coming!"

Eddie and Rachel rushed to Derek's side, pushing against the stone with all their might. It groaned and shifted, moving an inch, then another. One of the hooded figures broke from the circle and lunged toward them, but Derek grabbed a rock and hurled it at them, knocking them back.

Suddenly, a blast of cold air hit them like a wall, and they heard a deafening, inhuman screech that cut through the night. The figures seemed to recoil, their chant turning into a low, mournful wail.

"What was that?" Eddie shouted over the noise, panic in his eyes.

"It's the spirit," Rachel cried out, struggling to keep her footing as the wind whipped around

them. "It knows we're trying to stop it!"

They shoved the stone again, and this time, it tipped, crashing to the ground with a thundering boom. The moment it hit, the entire clearing seemed to shudder, the ground vibrating as if it were alive. The hooded figures screamed, their voices mingling with the inhuman wail, and several of them dropped to their knees, clutching their heads as if in pain.

But the chanting did not stop. The remaining figures raised their hands higher, their voices louder, more insistent. The symbols on the stones flared bright, glowing with an intense, blinding light that seemed to burn into their eyes.

"We need to break more of the circle!" Claire shouted, covering her face with her arm to shield herself from the light.

Derek grabbed another stone, but before he could move, a figure lunged at him, knocking him to the ground. He struggled, grappling with the hooded figure, and managed to roll on top, pinning them down. He ripped off the hood, revealing the pale, blank-eyed face of a young woman, her lips moving soundlessly.

Derek's heart skipped a beat. "She's not... she's not real," he realized aloud. "She's like Annie... a vessel."

Rachel grabbed another stone, using all her strength to push it over. As it fell, the light from the symbols flickered, and the wind intensified,

swirling violently around the clearing. The hooded figures seemed to glitch, their forms flickering, their faces distorted and shifting in the red glow of the flares.

Claire caught sight of movement at the edge of the clearing — a shadowy figure, tall and broad, its face obscured. She felt a wave of cold wash over her, her breath catching in her throat. "There's something else here," she whispered, her voice barely audible over the roaring wind. "Something... watching us."

Derek finally shoved the figure off him, scrambling to his feet. "Keep going!" he yelled. "Break them all!"

Rachel and Eddie moved to another stone, pushing against it with all their strength. The ground seemed to pulse beneath their feet, the mist swirling thicker, rising up to their waists. The chanting was louder than ever, almost a scream, and they felt the vibration in their bones.

Suddenly, the mist parted, and they saw it — a figure, tall and gaunt, its skin pale and stretched tight over its bones, its eyes hollow and black. It moved with a jerking, unnatural motion, its limbs long and thin, like it was being pulled by invisible strings.

Rachel's breath hitched in her throat. "Oh my God," she whispered. "What is that?"

Derek turned, and his blood ran cold. "That's... that's what they're calling," he said, his voice

barely above a whisper. "A guardian. A protector of the spirits."

The figure moved closer, its hollow eyes fixed on them, its mouth opening in a silent scream. The air grew colder, and they felt a deep, primal fear settle over them, paralyzing them in place.

"We have to keep moving!" Eddie shouted, his voice breaking through the fear. "Don't look at it! Just break the stones!"

With renewed determination, they pushed against the stones, one after another, toppling them over. Each time a stone fell, the light flickered, and the guardian let out a shriek, its form becoming more unstable, more distorted.

But it was getting closer, its long, skeletal fingers reaching out toward them. Rachel felt the cold brush of its touch on her skin, and she recoiled, feeling a deep, icy pain shoot through her arm.

"It's trying to take us," Claire shouted, her voice filled with panic. "We have to finish this... now!"

With one final push, they toppled the last stone. The circle was broken, and the symbols flickered and died, the light fading away. The chanting stopped abruptly, and the hooded figures collapsed to the ground, their bodies lifeless and still.

The guardian let out a final, ear-piercing scream, and then it too began to dissolve, its form breaking apart like smoke in the wind. The mist lifted, the wind died down, and the forest fell silent.

For a moment, they stood there, breathing heavily, their bodies trembling with adrenaline. "Is it... is it over?" Eddie asked, his voice barely a whisper.

But before anyone could answer, they heard it — a low, rumbling growl, deep and guttural, coming from the forest beyond. The ground began to tremble, and they felt a new presence, something even more powerful, more malevolent, rising from the darkness.

Derek's eyes widened in horror. "No," he whispered. "It's not over... we've only just begun."

CHAPTER 15: DESCENT INTO DARKNESS

The forest around them was alive with an unsettling energy, a palpable tension that thrummed through the air like a heartbeat. The rumbling growl they heard seemed to come from everywhere and nowhere, reverberating off the trees, bouncing back at them from the mist.

Derek's words hung in the air, heavy with dread: "It's not over... we've only just begun."

Claire's breath hitched in her throat, her hands instinctively gripping the flashlight tighter. She swept its beam across the trees, trying to pierce through the thick fog that was rapidly rolling in again. "Derek, what do we do?" she whispered, voice trembling. "What is coming?"

Derek didn't answer immediately. His eyes were fixed on the forest, his mind racing through the possibilities. He had seen many things in his years

of searching for the supernatural — things that defied logic, that pushed the boundaries of what he believed was possible. But this... this felt different. Darker. Stronger. Like they had just awakened something that was never meant to be disturbed.

Rachel's voice cut through the silence, taut with anxiety. "Derek, answer me! What's coming?"

Derek turned to face her, his expression grim. "I don't know," he admitted, his voice low. "But whatever it is, it's powerful. More powerful than anything I've ever encountered." He took a deep breath, trying to steady himself. "We need to get out of here. Now."

Eddie shook his head, wiping sweat from his brow despite the cold. "And go where, man? We're in the middle of the woods, on top of a cursed mountain. You think we can just walk away from this?"

The rumble grew louder, a vibration they could feel in their chests, in their bones. The ground beneath their feet seemed to tremble, as if something enormous was moving beneath the surface. The trees swayed, their branches creaking, groaning under an unseen pressure.

"We don't have a choice!" Derek shouted over the noise. "If we stay here, we're sitting ducks. We need to find shelter... somewhere we can regroup and figure out our next move."

Rachel glanced around, her eyes wide with fear.

"But where? There's nothing out here except trees and rocks."

Claire's gaze fell on the darkened trail leading deeper into the woods. "What about that path?" she asked. "It looks like it leads somewhere... maybe an old cabin or a mine shaft. Anything would be better than standing out here in the open."

Derek nodded, making a quick decision. "Okay, let's go. Stay close, and don't stray from the path. Whatever you do, don't look back."

They moved as one, huddled together, making their way down the narrow, winding trail. The fog thickened around them, swallowing the light from their flashlights, reducing visibility to just a few feet ahead. The rumbling continued, growing louder with every step, accompanied by the occasional snapping of branches and rustling of leaves — sounds that made it clear something was moving around them, stalking them.

Eddie's breathing was fast and shallow, his hands trembling as he held his flashlight. He had grown up listening to ghost stories and urban legends, but nothing had prepared him for this. His mind was racing, filled with images of the guardian they had just faced, its skeletal hands reaching for him, its hollow eyes staring into his soul.

"What if it's Headless Annie?" Eddie muttered, trying to keep his voice steady. "What if she's not alone?"

Rachel shot him a sharp look. "Don't talk like that," she hissed. "We don't need to be thinking about her right now. We have enough to worry about."

Claire's footsteps slowed as she considered Eddie's words. "But... he might be right," she said, her voice barely above a whisper. "If that ritual was meant to call her back... maybe it brought something else with it. Something worse."

Derek stopped abruptly, turning to face them. "We can't let our imaginations run wild," he said firmly. "Not now. We need to stay focused. Keep moving."

They continued down the path, the fog swirling around their legs like a living thing, tendrils of mist reaching up, curling around their ankles, pulling them deeper into the woods. The trees closed in around them, their branches arching overhead like skeletal fingers. The air grew colder, each breath misting in the dim light, and the sounds of the forest seemed to fade away, replaced by an oppressive silence.

The rumbling stopped, and for a moment, they all paused, listening. The quiet was deafening, an unnatural stillness that set their nerves on edge.

"What happened?" Rachel whispered. "Why did it stop?"

Derek's eyes darted around, searching for any sign of movement. "I don't know," he said, his voice tense. "Maybe it's waiting... watching us."

"Waiting for what?" Claire asked, her voice trembling.

A twig snapped behind them, and they all spun around, flashlights sweeping over the trees. The fog was thicker than ever, obscuring their view, and they saw nothing but shadows and the faint outline of branches.

"Move!" Derek urged, pushing them forward. "Keep going!"

They picked up their pace, almost jogging down the trail, their footsteps crunching on the gravel. The path wound deeper into the woods, the darkness pressing in on all sides. Rachel's heart pounded in her chest, her breaths coming in sharp, ragged gasps. Her mind kept drifting back to the ritual, to the symbols on the stones, to the guardian... to the thought of Annie, her headless form roaming the mountainside, searching for her next victim.

Eddie's voice cut through the darkness. "Do you hear that?" he whispered.

They all stopped, straining to listen. At first, there was nothing... just the sound of their own breathing. Then, faintly, from somewhere deep in the woods, they heard it: the soft, mournful sound of a woman crying.

Claire's face went pale. "Oh no," she murmured. "It's her... it's Annie."

Rachel felt a chill run down her spine. "No, no... it's a trick," she said quickly. "It has to be."

The crying grew louder, closer, a haunting, sorrowful wail that echoed through the trees. They felt the ground tremble beneath their feet again, a low, steady rumble that seemed to come from all directions.

Derek's jaw tightened. "We have to keep moving," he said, trying to sound confident. "Don't listen to it. Don't let it get inside your head."

But the crying continued, growing more desperate, more anguished. It filled their ears, seeped into their bones, tugging at their hearts with an overwhelming sense of sorrow and loss.

Eddie's eyes were wide with fear. "I can't... I can't take it," he muttered, covering his ears. "Make it stop... please, make it stop!"

Rachel grabbed his arm. "Eddie, focus!" she shouted. "Look at me! Stay with me!"

Eddie nodded, his eyes glazed with panic. "Okay... okay," he whispered, trying to steady himself.

Derek pushed forward, leading them down the path. "We're almost there," he promised, though he had no idea if it was true. "Just a little further..."

Then they saw it — a small, dilapidated cabin, barely visible through the fog. Its roof was sagging, the windows dark and broken, but it was shelter. A place to hide.

"There!" Claire shouted, relief flooding her voice. "Go, go!"

They ran the last few steps, reaching the cabin door just as the rumbling grew louder, more intense. Derek pushed the door open, and they all scrambled inside, slamming it shut behind them. They leaned against the door, breathing heavily, their hearts racing.

For a moment, there was silence. Then the crying stopped, replaced by a low, menacing growl, deep and guttural, that seemed to come from right outside the door.

Rachel's eyes widened with terror. "It's here," she whispered. "Whatever it is... it's here."

They heard the sound of footsteps outside, slow and deliberate, crunching on the gravel. The door shook, rattling on its hinges, and they felt a cold draft sweep through the room.

Derek looked around, searching for something to barricade the door. "Help me!" he shouted, grabbing a broken chair and wedging it against the handle.

Claire and Eddie grabbed pieces of broken furniture, piling them against the door, their hands trembling with fear. The footsteps stopped, and for a moment, there was an eerie, unnatural silence.

Then, without warning, the door burst open, sending the makeshift barricade flying. A wave of cold air washed over them, and they saw a figure standing in the doorway — tall, dark, its features obscured by the shadows.

Rachel screamed, stumbling back. "No... no... it can't be..."

The figure stepped forward, and they saw its face — pale, gaunt, its eyes hollow and empty. It was Annie... but different. Changed. Her head was back, but her eyes were black pits, her mouth twisted into a malevolent grin.

"Welcome," she whispered, her voice cold and hollow. "Welcome to my domain."

Derek grabbed a piece of wood, holding it like a weapon. "Stay back!" he shouted, his voice shaking. "We're not afraid of you!"

Annie's grin widened, and she laughed, a low, sinister sound that sent chills down their spines. Her laughter echoed off the cabin walls, seeming to come from every corner of the small, dark space. The room grew colder, the temperature dropping rapidly as if all the warmth had been sucked out of the air. Frost formed on the windows, spreading in spider-web patterns across the glass, and their breath became visible in the frigid air.

Eddie backed away, stumbling over a broken chair leg. "Derek, what do we do?" he shouted, panic seeping into his voice. He was shaking uncontrollably, his skin turning pale. "What does she want?"

Derek kept his eyes locked on Annie, gripping the piece of wood tighter. "She wants to scare us... to break us," he replied. "She feeds on fear. Don't give her what she wants."

But Annie's presence was overpowering. Her black eyes bore into each of them, her grin stretching unnaturally wide, her head tilting to an impossible angle. "You're all mine," she whispered, her voice a strange, echoing hiss that seemed to come from everywhere and nowhere. "You came to my mountain... and now, you will never leave."

Rachel felt her legs weaken, her knees buckling under the weight of that terrifying promise.

Memories flooded back to her — nights spent listening to her grandmother's ghost stories, warnings never to wander into the woods after dark. She had always laughed them off, never believing they could be true. But now, face-to-face with the living embodiment of one of those tales, she realized how wrong she had been.

Claire stepped forward, her face set in grim determination, even as fear gripped her heart. "You don't scare us, Annie," she said, trying to keep her voice steady. "You're just a ghost... just a story." But as she spoke, a shadow fell across her face, and she saw the truth in Annie's dark, empty eyes

— this was no mere ghost. This was something older, something darker, something filled with hatred and pain.

Annie's smile faded, and her face contorted into a mask of rage. "A story?" she spat, her voice rising to a shriek that seemed to shake the very walls of the cabin. "You think I'm just a story?" Her eyes flared with a dark fire, and she raised her hands, her fingers twisting into claws.

Suddenly, the cabin began to shake violently. The walls creaked, the floorboards groaned, and objects flew off the shelves, crashing to the ground. The very air seemed to pulse with malevolent energy, and the lights flickered wildly, plunging the room into darkness before coming back on in a weak, sputtering glow.

Derek moved quickly, pulling Claire and Rachel back, away from the door. "Get back!" he shouted. "We have to stick together!"

Eddie was still frozen in place, his eyes wide with terror, staring at Annie as if mesmerized. "She's not real... she can't be real," he muttered to himself over and over again.

"Snap out of it, Eddie!" Derek yelled. "Don't let her get inside your head!"

Annie's laughter filled the room again, but this time it was louder, more intense, almost hysterical. "Oh, I'm real," she said, her voice dripping with mockery. "I'm very, very real." She stepped forward, and the temperature plummeted even further, the frost thickening on the windows, creeping along the walls like icy fingers.

Suddenly, the door slammed shut behind her with a deafening bang, trapping them all inside. The rumbling returned, this time even louder, as if the very earth beneath the cabin was coming alive.

Dust fell from the ceiling, and the walls seemed to bend inward, pressing closer, as if the cabin itself was trying to crush them.

Claire grabbed Derek's arm, her voice frantic. "We have to get out of here!" she screamed. "We can't stay!"

Derek nodded, his mind racing. "There must be another way out," he said, his eyes darting around the room. "A window, a back door... something!"

But Annie moved to block their path, her grin returning, wider than ever. "There is no way out," she taunted. "Not for any of you."

Rachel's heart pounded in her chest. She felt like she was suffocating, the air growing thinner, colder. She looked at Annie, and suddenly, she felt a strange sensation in her chest — a tightness, a burning, as if something was trying to claw its way out. Her hand went to her heart, her eyes widening with pain. "Derek... I... I can't breathe," she gasped.

Annie's eyes flickered with amusement, and she took another step forward. "Feel it," she whispered. "Feel the fear... let it consume you."

Derek lunged at Annie, swinging the piece of wood, but it passed right through her, as if she were made of smoke. She laughed again, her form wavering like a mirage, and Derek stumbled back, off balance.

Claire grabbed a chair leg and threw it at Annie, but it, too, went through her, clattering to the floor on the other side. "Damn it!" she shouted, her frustration boiling over. "What do we do? How do we fight her?"

Annie's laughter echoed off the walls, louder and louder, until it became almost unbearable. "You don't fight me," she said, her voice a cruel whisper. "You surrender... or you die."

Derek's mind raced, searching for something — anything — that could help them. He thought of the symbols, the ritual, the guardian they had faced. "The ritual... maybe we can reverse it," he muttered under his breath. "Send her back... seal her away."

Eddie's eyes snapped up. "How?" he asked, his voice desperate. "What do we need?"

Derek tried to remember, his thoughts scattered. "The symbols... we need to find them, redraw them... and we need something of hers, something that belongs to her."

Annie's expression darkened. "You think you can send me back?" she snarled. "You think I'll let you?"

The rumbling grew even louder, the walls shaking violently. The ground beneath their feet began to crack, and they could see the dark, churning earth beneath.

Rachel took a deep breath, trying to steady herself, trying to think. "Her locket," she said suddenly. "The one in the legend... it was buried with her.

It's supposed to be the source of her power."

Claire's eyes lit up with hope. "Then we need to find it," she said. "It must be here somewhere... buried in the cabin, maybe?"

Annie's face contorted with rage. "You will not find it!" she shrieked. "You will never find it!"

Derek took a step forward, his eyes locked on Annie. "We'll see about that," he said, his voice filled with determination. "We're not afraid of you."

Annie hissed, her form flickering, and the room grew darker, the shadows lengthening, closing in around them. "You should be," she whispered. "You all should be."

The ground trembled violently, and the cabin seemed to shrink, the walls pressing closer, the ceiling lowering, the air growing colder and thinner with every passing second. But despite the terror clawing at their hearts, Derek, Claire, Rachel, and Eddie stood their ground, their faces set with determination.

They were going to fight. They were going to find the locket. And they were going to send Headless Annie back to whatever dark place she had come from — or die trying.

Chapter 16: The Ritual of the Dead

The cabin was a trap, the walls seeming to pulse and breathe with a malevolent life of their own. Outside, the wind howled like a chorus of tormented souls, slamming against the rotting wooden walls and shaking the foundation. Inside, the four of them huddled together, their breaths coming out in cold puffs, the frost creeping along the floor, inching ever closer to their feet.

Derek felt the weight of the task bearing down on him like a physical force. "We need to find that locket," he repeated, trying to focus his mind. His hands shook as he clutched the piece of wood tighter, his knuckles white with the effort. He glanced at Rachel, who was rubbing her arms, trying to stave off the cold. "Rachel, think—where would they have buried it?"

Rachel's mind was spinning. She tried to recall every scrap of folklore her grandmother had told her, every word that might hold a clue. "It... it would have to be somewhere close," she muttered, almost to herself. "The story says the locket was buried with her, near where she died. If we're right and this cabin is some kind of focus for her spirit, then maybe it's here, somewhere hidden, somewhere we haven't looked yet."

Eddie's teeth chattered as he spoke. "This place is a tomb," he said, glancing nervously at the dark corners of the room, half-expecting to see Annie emerge from the shadows. "Why would they bury her locket in a place like this?"

"Because it's a prison," Claire replied, her eyes scanning the floorboards for any sign of a hidden compartment or trap-door. "If the locket holds her power, they would have wanted it somewhere she couldn't escape from. But... they didn't do a good enough job."

Annie's laughter filled the air again, a low, mocking chuckle that seemed to come from

everywhere at once. "You think you're so clever," she sneered, her voice wrapping around them like a vice. "But you'll never find it. You'll never be free of me."

Derek ignored her, forcing himself to focus. "We need to find it now," he insisted, his voice steadier than he felt. "Start looking—tear this place apart if you have to."

Rachel dropped to her knees, scraping at the floor with her fingers, searching for any loose boards or hidden compartments. Claire moved to the walls, running her hands over the rough, decaying wood, feeling for any hollow spots. Eddie, still shaking, began to dig through the piles of debris scattered across the floor, his hands numb with cold.

Minutes ticked by, feeling like hours, the air growing colder, the darkness deeper. The tension was suffocating, the cabin closing in on them, and still, there was no sign of the locket.

Suddenly, Rachel stopped, her hand brushing against something metallic buried beneath a layer of dust and grime. "Wait!" she shouted, her voice trembling with excitement. "I think I found something!" She frantically cleared the dirt away, revealing a small iron ring set into one of the floorboards.

Derek was at her side in an instant. "What is it?" he asked, his voice taut with urgency.

"A trapdoor, maybe?" Rachel replied, tugging on the ring. It creaked, resisting her efforts, but she

pulled harder, putting her weight into it. With a loud groan, the floorboard lifted, revealing a dark, narrow space beneath.

Claire grabbed a flashlight from her bag and shone it into the hole. The beam illuminated a set of wooden steps, leading down into a deeper darkness. "Looks like some kind of cellar," she said, her voice hushed. "Think it's down there?"

"There's only one way to find out," Derek replied grimly. He took a deep breath, then started down the steps, the others following close behind.

The cellar was pitch black, the air heavy with the smell of damp earth and decay. The flashlight's beam danced across the dirt floor, revealing old crates, rusted tools, and cobwebs that hung like drapes. The space felt wrong, the atmosphere thick with an unnatural presence, and their footsteps echoed strangely, as if swallowed by the dark.

"Stay close," Derek whispered, his eyes darting around. "And keep your eyes open."

They moved cautiously, every creak and groan of the old wood sending jolts of fear through them. Rachel felt a cold draft brush against her neck, and she spun around, half-expecting to see Annie's ghastly figure behind her. But there was nothing — just shadows and the oppressive darkness.

Eddie trailed behind, his heart hammering in his chest. His childhood fear of the dark resurfaced, amplified by the sense of dread that permeated the air. He tried to steady his breathing, to remind

himself that they had a plan. But a voice in the back of his mind whispered that it wouldn't be enough, that they were doomed no matter what they did.

As they pressed on, Derek's flashlight caught a glimpse of something on the far wall — a small, ornate box, half-buried in the dirt. His heart leaped in his chest. "There," he said, pointing. "That might be it!"

Claire hurried over, reaching out to grab the box, but as her fingers brushed against it, the cellar seemed to shift. The walls groaned, and the floor trembled, a low, rumbling sound filling the air.

Annie's voice echoed around them, cold and triumphant. "You're getting closer," she sang, her tone taunting. "But you'll never make it out alive."

Rachel grabbed Claire's arm, pulling her back. "Careful!" she warned. "It could be trapped!"

Derek nodded. "She's trying to scare us, trying to make us panic," he said, though his own voice was tight with fear. "Stay calm. We can do this."

Claire, more determined than ever, took a deep breath and reached for the box again. This time, she lifted it slowly, cautiously, feeling its weight. It was cold to the touch, and a strange energy seemed to pulse from within it.

Suddenly, the ground shook violently, and a deep crack appeared in the floor, spreading toward them like a jagged wound. Dirt and debris fell from the ceiling, and the air filled with dust.

"We need to move!" Derek shouted. "Get back upstairs, now!"

They turned and sprinted back up the steps, the rumbling growing louder, the very foundation of the cabin seeming to come apart around them.

Claire clutched the box tightly to her chest, her heart pounding.

As they reached the top of the stairs, the cellar door slammed shut behind them with a deafening bang. Annie's laughter filled the air again, louder, more manic than before.

"You think you're safe?" she cackled. "You think that will help you?"

Derek took the box from Claire, his hands trembling. "We need to open it," he said urgently. "See if the locket is inside."

Rachel grabbed a knife from the table and handed it to him. "Careful," she whispered. "We don't know what else might be in there."

Derek nodded and carefully pried the box open. Inside, lying on a bed of faded velvet, was a small, silver locket, tarnished with age. His breath caught in his throat. "This is it," he said softly. "This has to be it."

But as soon as his fingers touched the locket, a wave of cold shot through his body, and he felt something dark and malicious clawing at his mind. Images flashed before his eyes — the couple lost in the fog, the truck driver's bloody glove, the teenagers' terrified last moments. He heard their screams, felt their fear, and he knew Annie was

showing him what awaited them.

"No!" he shouted, pulling his hand away, breaking the connection. He staggered back, his face pale, his breathing ragged.

Rachel moved to his side, her eyes wide with concern. "Derek, are you okay?" she asked, but before he could answer, the cabin walls began to bend inward again, the floor cracking open like the earth was trying to swallow them whole.

"We have to finish the ritual," Claire said, her voice urgent. "Before she stops us. Before... before it's too late."

Derek nodded, trying to steady himself. "We'll need the symbols... the ones we saw before," he said, his mind racing. "They must be part of the ritual to seal her away."

Eddie looked around frantically. "There's no time!" he shouted. "She's not going to let us—"

Annie's figure materialized before them, her headless body standing at the center of the room. "You think you can stop me?" she hissed, her voice a low, angry growl. "You think you can escape my curse?"

Claire stepped forward, holding the locket high, as if it were a weapon. "We're not afraid of you, Annie!" she yelled, her voice defiant. "We're going to send you back where you belong!"

Annie shrieked, a sound so piercing it felt like knives driving into their ears. The room shook violently, objects flying through the air, the

windows shattering inward, and a deafening roar filling their senses.

But Derek stood firm, focusing on the symbols, the locket, the ritual — everything they had learned. "We're going to end this," he muttered, more to himself than anyone else. "We're going to end this... or die trying."

Chapter 17: The Battle with Shadows

The cabin quaked around them as if possessed by Annie's fury, each creak and groan echoing her rage. Dust cascaded from the rafters like a deathly mist, swirling through the icy air. The dim light from their flashlights flickered wildly, casting long, erratic shadows across the walls, shadows that seemed to move and writhe of their own volition.

Derek tightened his grip on the silver locket. He could feel the energy radiating from it, an ancient power humming just beneath the surface, both a key to their salvation and a conduit to something far darker. The cold metal pulsed in his hand like a beating heart, and he knew their time was running out.

Rachel turned to him, her face a mask of determination, though her eyes betrayed a deep- seated fear. "We need to finish the ritual," she urged, her voice barely audible over the chaos. "Whatever you saw, whatever you felt, we have to use it."

Derek nodded, swallowing his fear. "The symbols," he whispered. "We need to recreate the symbols, the ones we saw in the visions, the ones etched in blood and earth. They're the key to binding her... or breaking free."

Claire quickly began to search through her bag, her hands shaking, pulling out chalk, salt, and other items they had brought. "I remember some of them," she said, her voice strained but steady. "But we have to be exact. Any mistake, and it could make things worse."

"Worse?" Eddie scoffed nervously, his eyes darting around the room, expecting Annie's headless figure to emerge from any corner. "How could this get any worse?"

But even as he spoke, the walls seemed to ripple, the shadows on them stretching, twisting, growing darker. Shapes began to form within the shadows

— grotesque, disfigured, elongated limbs reaching out toward them, a cacophony of whispers and muttered curses filling the room.

Rachel's heart pounded in her chest, and she bit down on her lip to steady herself. Her childhood memories of listening to her grandmother's ghost stories came rushing back, the tales of spirits and demons, of curses and dark magic. She had never truly believed in them... until now. Now, she felt as if she were living those very stories, trapped in a nightmare that defied all reason.

"We have to stay focused," she murmured, almost to herself. "We have to stay together."

Derek nodded, crouching down to draw the first symbol on the floor with the chalk. His hand trembled, but he forced himself to be precise, to remember every detail from his vision — the way the lines curved, the intersecting angles, the ancient markings that seemed to pulse with an otherworldly energy.

Claire followed his lead, working quickly beside him, her movements careful and deliberate. She could feel the malevolence thick in the air, pressing down on her like a weight. Every nerve in her body screamed at her to run, to get out of this cursed place, but she forced herself to stay, to fight.

Eddie watched them work, his breath coming in short, ragged bursts. His fear of the dark had been his constant companion since he was a child, a silent terror that had always loomed just beyond the edges of his vision. But this darkness was different. It was alive, malevolent, reaching for him with cold, grasping hands. He felt it trying to crawl inside his mind, whispering his deepest fears, his darkest thoughts.

"Eddie," Rachel called, sensing his rising panic. "We need you. We need you to stay with us."

He nodded, swallowing hard, forcing himself to move closer to the group, closer to the dim glow of the flashlight. "I'm here," he whispered, though he felt anything but present. His heart was racing, every instinct screaming at him to flee.

Annie's voice cut through the air again, filled with mockery and venom. "You think your little drawings will save you?" she hissed. "You think you can bind me with symbols and spells? You are mine. You have always been mine."

The temperature in the room dropped even further, their breaths coming out in short, visible puffs.

Derek glanced around, sensing the shift in the air, feeling Annie's power growing stronger. He pushed himself to work faster, drawing the final symbol with desperate urgency.

Claire finished her section and began to sprinkle salt along the lines, chanting softly under her breath, invoking the protection spells she had studied, the old incantations her grandmother had taught her. She wasn't sure if they would work, but it was all they had, and she was willing to try anything.

Suddenly, the symbols on the floor began to glow, a faint, eerie light emanating from the chalk lines. The shadows recoiled slightly, the tendrils pulling back, hesitating. For a brief moment, there was a glimmer of hope.

"We're doing it!" Rachel exclaimed, feeling a surge of adrenaline. "It's working!"

But then, the light flickered, dimmed, and the shadows surged forward again, more aggressively this time, like a wave crashing against a fragile dam. The ground beneath them trembled, and a low, guttural growl filled the air, vibrating through their bones.

Derek gritted his teeth, holding the locket up, trying to channel his thoughts, his will, into it. "Annie!" he shouted, his voice breaking through the cacophony. "This ends now! We have your locket. We know your secret. We know your pain!"

The laughter stopped, replaced by a sudden, chilling silence. The shadows stilled, as if waiting, listening.

"You don't know my pain," Annie's voice replied, softer now, tinged with an emotion they hadn't heard before. Was it... sadness?

Derek hesitated, sensing a shift in her tone. "Tell us, Annie," he continued, carefully. "Tell us what happened. Why are you here? Why do you torment these roads?"

The shadows seemed to ripple, wavering as if uncertain. And then, from the darkness, they saw her — Annie's ghostly figure, still headless, but now less threatening, more mournful. Her form flickered, like a candle struggling against the wind.

"Why do you care?" she whispered, her voice barely more than a breath. "Why would you care about what happened to me?"

Rachel stepped forward, her heart pounding, but her voice steady. "Because we want to help you," she said. "We want to end this... to set you free."

Annie's figure hesitated, and for a moment, they thought they saw a faint outline of a face where her head should have been, a young woman's face, pale and drawn, eyes wide with fear and longing.

"They took everything from me," Annie murmured, her voice filled with a sorrow so deep it seemed to vibrate through the air. "They took my life, my love... and they left me to wander this mountain, searching... always searching..."

Eddie felt a pang of empathy, his fear momentarily overshadowed by a deep, aching sadness. "Searching for what?" he asked softly. "What are you looking for?"

"My head," she replied, her voice breaking. "They took my head... and with it, my peace. I cannot rest until I am whole again."

The revelation hung in the air, and they all felt the weight of her words. Annie wasn't just a vengeful spirit — she was a soul trapped in torment, caught in a cycle of endless searching, unable to move on.

Derek held up the locket again, his mind racing. "Is this what connects you to this place?" he asked. "Is this what binds you here?"

Annie's figure seemed to shimmer, her form becoming less distinct. "It... it holds my memory," she whispered. "But it is not what I seek. It is a piece of me, but not enough..."

Rachel glanced at the others, a new determination in her eyes. "Then we'll help you find it," she declared. "We'll find your head. We'll help you put an end to this."

Annie's form flickered, and for the briefest moment, they saw her smile, a sad, wistful smile. "You would do that... for me?" she asked, her

voice filled with a mixture of disbelief and hope.

Derek nodded, his fear momentarily replaced by compassion. "Yes," he said firmly. "We will help you... if you promise to let us go, and to never hurt anyone again."

Annie's figure seemed to waver, her ghostly presence growing fainter. "I... I will try," she murmured, her voice fading. "But hurry... I can feel the darkness pulling at me... I don't know how much longer I can hold it back..."

And then, just like that, she was gone, her presence dissipating into the air, leaving them in the cold, eerie silence of the cabin once more.

The shadows seemed to retreat, shrinking back into the corners, and the room grew still. For a

moment, they all just stood there, catching their breath, trying to process what had just happened.

"We need to find her head," Rachel said quietly, breaking the silence. "We need to find it before it's too late."

Derek nodded, feeling the weight of their task settling on his shoulders. "And we need to do it fast," he agreed. "Because if we don't... we might not get another chance."

Eddie looked around, his fear still palpable but tempered now by a sense of purpose. "Where do we even start?" he asked, his voice trembling

Chapter 18: The Descent into Darkness

The cabin walls seemed to breathe a sigh of relief as Annie's presence dissipated, but the room remained thick with tension. The air was still cold, and the shadows lingered, watching, waiting. The gravity of what they had just promised settled over them like a shroud. Derek, Rachel, Claire, and Eddie stood in a tight circle, each of them feeling the weight of Annie's final, desperate words.

"We need to find her head," Rachel repeated, more to herself than to the others. Her voice was steady, but her eyes betrayed a flicker of doubt. "But where do we even begin?"

Derek wiped a sheen of sweat from his forehead, his breath fogging in the cold air. "We've been looking in the wrong places," he muttered, thinking aloud. "If her head is what binds her here, then it has to be somewhere significant.

Somewhere tied to the original ritual that trapped her. Somewhere hidden, or protected."

Claire's eyes widened, and she turned to Derek with a sudden realization. "The mountain," she whispered. "Remember the stories? The old burial grounds? The settlers... they believed the mountain itself had power. If Annie's head was separated from her body, it might be buried there... somewhere near the old grounds, somewhere that they believed would contain her spirit forever."

Rachel nodded, feeling a surge of determination. "That makes sense," she said. "They would have hidden it somewhere no one would think to look,

somewhere they thought was sacred or cursed... somewhere no one would dare disturb."

Eddie's face paled, the blood draining from his cheeks. "You're talking about the old mining caves," he stammered. "The ones they sealed up decades ago, after the collapses... after the stories started spreading. People said they heard voices, saw shadows... things that shouldn't have been there."

Derek exchanged a glance with Rachel. "That's where we're going," he decided, his voice firm. "We don't have much time. Annie's barely holding herself back, and if we don't act fast, we might not get another chance."

The group gathered their gear quickly, stuffing flashlights, ropes, and other supplies into their bags. The air was thick with urgency, and every second felt like a countdown toward some unknown, inevitable catastrophe.

As they stepped outside, the night air was frigid and biting, the wind howling through the trees like a chorus of wails. The moon hung low in the sky, casting an eerie, silvery light across the landscape, illuminating the jagged silhouette of the mountain in the distance. The dark, hulking shape seemed to loom over them, a brooding presence filled with secrets and shadows.

"We'll have to hike to the base," Derek said, leading the way. "From there, we'll find the old trail that leads to the mines."

The path was narrow and treacherous, overgrown with roots and brambles, the forest closing in around them like a living thing. Every rustle of leaves, every snap of a twig, sent jolts of fear through their bodies. Their breaths came in ragged puffs, visible in the cold air.

Eddie's nerves were on edge. He kept glancing over his shoulder, half-expecting to see Annie's headless form gliding silently behind them. "This place... it doesn't feel right," he muttered, his voice barely above a whisper. "Like it's watching us... waiting."

Claire tried to calm him down, though her own hands were shaking. "It's just the wind," she said, though she wasn't sure if she believed it herself. "We're in the woods at night... of course, it feels creepy."

Rachel led the group, her flashlight cutting through the darkness. She could feel something out there

— an unseen presence, a malevolent force lurking just beyond the reach of the light. The forest seemed to breathe, each gust of wind a low, mournful sigh.

Suddenly, Derek stopped, holding up a hand. "Quiet," he whispered. "Do you hear that?"

They all paused, straining to listen. At first, there was only the sound of the wind through the trees, but then... faintly, almost imperceptibly, they heard it — a distant, rhythmic pounding, like the slow, steady beat of a drum.

"What is that?" Eddie whispered, his eyes wide with fear.

"The mines," Claire replied, her voice trembling. "The old miners used to signal with knocks... but that's impossible. The mines have been abandoned for decades. There shouldn't be anyone down there."

Derek's jaw clenched. "We're not alone," he said grimly. "Keep moving."

They pressed on, the pounding growing louder with each step, reverberating through the ground, vibrating in their bones. The air grew colder, and a thick fog began to seep through the trees, curling around their ankles like tendrils of smoke.

After what felt like an eternity, they reached the base of the mountain. The entrance to the old mining caves loomed before them, a gaping black maw cut into the rock. The metal gate that once barred the entrance hung open, rusted and broken, creaking in the wind.

"Here we are," Derek said, taking a deep breath. "Everyone ready?"

Eddie's hands were trembling, but he nodded. "Let's do this," he said, though his voice quavered with fear.

Rachel stepped forward, shining her flashlight into the darkness of the cave. "Stay close," she advised, her voice taut. "And whatever you do, don't wander off."

They stepped into the cave, their footsteps echoing off the stone walls. The air was thick with dust, and the smell of damp earth and decay filled their nostrils. The darkness was suffocating, pressing in on them from all sides.

As they moved deeper, the rhythmic pounding grew louder, more insistent, like the heartbeat of the mountain itself. The walls seemed to close in around them, the passages narrowing, twisting, leading them deeper into the earth.

Derek's flashlight flickered, the beam wavering. "Stay calm," he murmured, though his heart was racing. "It's just old batteries... we're fine."

But then, a sudden gust of wind rushed through the tunnel, snuffing out their flashlights in an instant, plunging them into complete darkness. The pounding stopped, replaced by a deafening silence.

Panic surged through them, breaths coming fast and shallow. "What's happening?" Eddie gasped, his voice tight with fear. "Why can't I see?"

"Hold on," Claire whispered, fumbling with her flashlight. She clicked it repeatedly, but nothing happened. "No... no, no, no... it was working just a second ago!"

A low, deep chuckle echoed through the cave, and they all froze. It was a sound unlike any they had ever heard — not quite human, not quite animal, a guttural, rasping noise that seemed to come from everywhere at once.

Derek's heart pounded in his chest. "Stick together," he ordered, reaching out to grab

Rachel's arm. "Don't let go of each other. We move as one."

They linked hands in the dark, moving forward slowly, cautiously. The darkness seemed alive, pressing against their skin, whispering in their ears. The walls felt as though they were breathing, and the air was thick with the scent of decay and something far worse — something foul and ancient.

Suddenly, Claire gasped, yanking her hand away. "Something touched me!" she cried, her voice rising in panic. "Something cold and wet... it was like a hand!"

Eddie's grip tightened on Derek's arm, his voice breaking. "We need to get out of here," he urged. "This is wrong... this is all wrong!"

Rachel forced herself to stay calm, though fear clawed at her insides. "Keep moving," she insisted. "We're close. I can feel it... Annie's head is here. It has to be."

They pressed on, moving deeper into the cave. The tunnel sloped downward, the air growing colder with each step. Derek's foot hit something soft, and he nearly stumbled. He knelt down, reaching out cautiously, and his fingers brushed against fabric — old, decaying cloth, covered in dust and grime.

"What is it?" Rachel asked, her voice tense.

Derek swallowed hard. "A coat," he whispered. "An old miner's coat... someone's been here."

Eddie's breath hitched in his throat. "We need to hurry," he said, his voice almost a whimper. "We need to find it and get out."

They moved faster, urgency driving them forward. The darkness seemed to grow thicker, more oppressive. The air was frigid now, each breath burning in their lungs. The tunnel opened into a larger chamber, and they found themselves standing at the edge of a vast underground pit.

A strange, bluish light flickered at the bottom, casting eerie shadows on the walls. And there, in the center of the pit, stood an old wooden altar, covered in strange symbols and markings, stained with something dark and dried.

Rachel's heart pounded in her chest as she approached the edge, peering down. "Look!" she whispered, pointing. "There... on the altar!"

Derek followed her gaze, and his breath caught in his throat. Resting on the altar, surrounded by a circle of stones, was a skull — old, yellowed, its empty eye sockets staring up at them.

Annie's head.

"We found it," Claire breathed, her voice filled with awe and fear. "We actually found it…"

But before they could move closer, a deep, rumbling growl erupted from the shadows around them, reverberating through the cavern like thunder. The ground trembled beneath their feet, small stones skittering and rolling down into the pit. The bluish light flickered violently, almost as if

it were fighting to stay alive against some invisible force.

Derek turned sharply, his eyes scanning the darkness that surrounded them. The growl was unlike anything he'd ever heard — low, guttural, and filled with a fury that sent chills down his spine. "Get ready!" he shouted, his voice echoing off the walls. "Something's coming!"

Rachel grabbed his arm, her face pale but determined. "We have to get the head," she insisted. "We're so close, Derek! If we leave now, we'll never have another chance."

Eddie was already backing away, his eyes wide with terror. "Are you out of your mind?" he cried, his voice breaking. "Did you hear that? We need to get out of here before whatever that is gets to us!"

Claire was torn, her gaze flicking between the skull on the altar and the darkness that seemed to close in around them like a vice. She felt a sudden wave of nausea wash over her, her skin prickling with fear. "Derek… Rachel… maybe he's right," she whispered, her voice shaking. "Maybe we should…"

Before she could finish, a shape began to emerge from the shadows. It was massive, hunched, and vaguely humanoid, but its proportions were all wrong — too long, too thin, with limbs that seemed to bend in unnatural directions. Its skin was a mottled gray, covered in dark patches that glistened wetly in the faint light. Its face was obscured by the darkness, but they could see the

gleam of its eyes — two pinpricks of red light that stared at them with a hunger that was almost palpable.

Rachel felt a scream rising in her throat, but she swallowed it down, her hand tightening on Derek's arm. "We have to move!" she hissed. "Now!"

Derek nodded, his heart hammering in his chest. "We go down," he said, his voice firm. "We get the head and we end this. If we don't, we're all dead anyway."

Eddie let out a strangled laugh, his fear turning to hysteria. "Down there? Are you insane?"

Derek ignored him, grabbing a length of rope from his pack and quickly tying it around a nearby stalagmite. "Claire, help me secure this," he ordered. "Rachel, you and Eddie keep an eye on that... thing."

Rachel nodded, turning to face the creature, which was now moving slowly toward them, its movements slow and deliberate, almost as if it were testing them, gauging their reaction. Her hands trembled, but she steadied herself, lifting her flashlight and pointing it directly at the creature's face.

The beam of light hit it full on, and for a moment, they caught a glimpse of its features — sunken cheeks, skin stretched tight over a skeletal frame, and a mouth filled with rows of jagged, broken teeth. The creature let out a low, hissing sound, recoiling slightly, but it did not retreat. Instead, it

seemed to grow bolder, its eyes narrowing as it continued its slow advance.

"Derek, hurry!" Rachel urged, her voice strained.

Derek finished securing the rope and tossed the end over the edge of the pit. "I'll go first," he said. "Cover me!"

He grabbed the rope and swung himself over the side, descending quickly into the darkness below. The rope burned his hands, the rough fibers cutting into his skin, but he didn't slow down. He could feel the weight of time pressing against him, the knowledge that they had only moments before the creature reached them.

Rachel and Claire watched with bated breath as Derek made his way down. The creature paused, its head tilting as if considering its next move.

Then, with a sudden burst of speed, it lunged forward, closing the distance between them in an instant.

"Eddie, throw me the salt!" Rachel shouted, reaching out her hand.

Eddie fumbled with his bag, pulling out a small vial of salt and tossing it to her. Rachel caught it and quickly scattered a line of salt across the ground between them and the creature. For a brief moment, the creature hesitated, its movements jerky and uncertain.

"It's working!" Claire shouted, her voice filled with a mix of relief and disbelief. "It's actually working!"

But the moment of reprieve was short-lived. The creature let out a roar, a deafening, bone-chilling sound that seemed to shake the very walls of the cavern. It swiped a long, clawed hand at the salt line, scattering it into the air, and continued its advance, more determined than ever.

"Damn it!" Rachel cursed. "We need more time!"

Derek reached the bottom of the pit, landing with a thud on the rocky ground. He looked up, seeing the creature bearing down on them, and felt a surge of panic. "Rachel! Claire! Keep it distracted!" he shouted, sprinting toward the altar.

The closer he got, the colder the air became, a frigid wind swirling around him, tugging at his clothes, biting at his skin. He reached the altar, his breath coming in short, sharp gasps, and grabbed the skull, feeling its icy weight in his hands.

The moment his fingers closed around it, the ground beneath him shook violently. A low, mournful wail filled the air, and the bluish light intensified, casting grotesque shadows on the walls. Derek felt a surge of energy pulse through the skull, a dark, malevolent force that seemed to seep into his very bones.

"Derek, hurry!" Rachel screamed from above, her voice filled with fear. "It's getting closer!"

Derek turned, cradling the skull to his chest. He ran back to the rope, his heart pounding, his breath ragged. As he reached for the rope, he felt something cold wrap around his ankle. He looked

down and saw a hand — pale, skeletal, clawed — gripping him tightly, pulling him back.

"No!" he shouted, kicking at the hand, trying to free himself. But the grip only tightened, pulling him down, dragging him away from the rope.

Above him, Rachel and Claire screamed his name, their voices echoing through the cavern. Derek struggled, kicking and thrashing, but the hand was impossibly strong, and it was pulling him toward the darkness.

"Derek!" Rachel shouted, leaning over the edge, her flashlight beam dancing wildly in the darkness. "Hold on! We're coming!"

Eddie grabbed another length of rope and tied it around his waist. "I'll go down," he muttered, his face pale but resolute. "I can't let him... I can't..."

But before he could descend, another hand shot out from the shadows, grabbing hold of his ankle and yanking him backward. Eddie screamed, falling to the ground, kicking wildly.

Rachel grabbed the rope, ready to go after Derek, but Claire stopped her, her eyes wide with terror. "Wait! Look!"

From the darkness, more shapes began to emerge — dozens of them, hunched and twisted, their eyes glowing like embers in the dark. They moved slowly at first, but then with increasing speed, closing in from all sides.

"We're surrounded!" Claire cried, her voice filled with despair. "There are too many of them!"

Derek's heart raced as he struggled against the hand holding him, feeling the pull of the darkness growing stronger. "Rachel! Get out of here!" he shouted, his voice breaking. "Get out while you can!"

Rachel shook her head fiercely, tears streaming down her face. "No! I'm not leaving you!"

Derek felt the darkness creeping into his mind, cold and relentless. He knew he was running out of time. "Please, Rachel... go..." he whispered, his voice barely audible. "Before it's too late..."

But Rachel was already moving, her determination unwavering. She gripped the rope and slid down into the pit, her eyes locked on Derek, her heart pounding with fear and resolve. She wouldn't leave him — not now, not ever.

As she reached the bottom, she felt the ground shake beneath her feet, the air thick with a sense of impending doom. The shadows seemed to close in around them, whispering, muttering, reaching.

Derek looked up, his face pale and drawn. "Rachel... you shouldn't have come," he whispered, his voice filled with a mixture of fear and gratitude.

Rachel smiled, a sad, determined smile. "I couldn't leave you," she replied, her voice steady. "We're in this together... until the end."

She reached out and grabbed his hand, pulling him up. The moment their fingers touched, the cold seemed to retreat slightly, the shadows wavering as

if uncertain. For a brief moment, they felt a flicker of hope.

But then, the growl returned, louder and more furious than before, and the creature lunged forward, its claws outstretched, its eyes burning with rage. The others were following, a horde of twisted, shadowy figures rushing toward them like a wave.

Rachel tightened her grip on Derek's hand. "We run," she said simply. "We run like hell."

And together, they ran, the skull clutched tightly in Derek's arms, the darkness closing in around them. They could feel the creatures at their heels, their breath hot and rancid, their claws reaching out, grasping

Derek and Rachel sprinted through the cavern, their feet pounding on the cold, uneven ground. Each step felt like a race against death itself, the air thick with fear and adrenaline. The shadows around them seemed to pulse, to breathe, their whispers growing louder and more frantic with every second.

Derek glanced back over his shoulder and saw the creatures gaining on them, their long, skeletal limbs moving with an unnatural speed. Their eyes burned like coals, their mouths open in silent screams, as if they were driven by some primal hunger that would never be satisfied.

"Faster!" Rachel shouted, her voice taut with desperation. "We have to go faster!"

But the pit floor was slick and uneven, covered with jagged rocks and loose gravel. Rachel's foot slipped, and she stumbled, nearly falling to the ground. Derek caught her, pulling her back up, his grip firm and steady. "I've got you," he muttered, his breath coming in sharp, ragged bursts. "Just keep moving!"

Ahead of them, the tunnel narrowed, the walls closing in like the jaws of a giant beast. The air was thick with dust and the smell of decay, and their lungs burned with each breath. The creatures were almost upon them now, their guttural growls filling the air, the sound of claws scraping against stone echoing around them like a sinister symphony.

"There's the rope!" Derek shouted, pointing to where the rope hung down from the ledge above, swaying gently in the faint breeze. "We just need to reach it!"

Rachel nodded, her eyes fixed on their only escape. "Go!" she urged, her voice raw. "I'll cover you!"

Derek hesitated for just a fraction of a second, torn between the need to protect her and the urgency to get the skull out of this hellish place. But Rachel's fierce determination left no room for argument. He nodded and sprinted toward the rope, gripping it tightly in his hands.

As he began to climb, Rachel turned to face the oncoming horde, her flashlight beam cutting through the darkness. She fumbled in her pocket for the small vial of holy water she had brought with her, her fingers shaking as she unscrewed the cap. "Stay back!" she shouted, her voice filled with a defiant courage. "Stay back, or I'll use this!"

For a moment, the creatures hesitated, their red eyes narrowing, their movements uncertain. The one at the front snarled, its lips peeling back to reveal rows of jagged, blackened teeth. It hissed, a sound like steam escaping from a kettle, and stepped closer.

Rachel flung a few drops of holy water toward it, the liquid shimmering in the dim light. The creature recoiled, a scream of rage and pain tearing from its throat as the water sizzled against its flesh, smoke rising where the drops had landed. The others shrieked in response, a cacophony of furious cries that sent shivers down her spine.

"Rachel, hurry!" Derek shouted from above, already halfway up the rope. "I can't hold it for long!"

Rachel backed toward the rope, her hand still tightly clutching the vial. She threw more holy water at the approaching figures, each splash causing them to shriek and recoil, but they were undeterred. There were too many of them, and they were closing in fast.

Claire and Eddie, still up above, reached down with desperate hands. "Rachel, jump!" Eddie

yelled, leaning over the edge as far as he dared. "We'll catch you!"

Rachel turned, grabbed the rope, and began to climb, her muscles screaming in protest, every pull on the rope feeling like it might be her last. The creatures were just below her, their claws scraping against the rock, reaching up, trying to drag her back down into the abyss.

Derek reached the top and turned, extending a hand to help pull her up. "Come on, Rachel! Almost there!"

But just as Rachel reached up for Derek's hand, a cold, skeletal grip closed around her ankle. She gasped, looking down to see one of the creatures clinging to her leg, its face twisted into a hideous snarl, its eyes blazing with fury.

"Derek!" she screamed, kicking wildly, trying to free herself. "Help me!"

Derek grabbed her wrist and pulled with all his strength, his muscles straining, his face contorted with effort. "Hold on!" he grunted. "I've got you!"

The creature hissed, tightening its grip, dragging Rachel down inch by inch. She could feel its claws digging into her flesh, cold and sharp, like ice-cold knives cutting through her skin. Panic surged through her, and she kicked harder, her foot connecting with its face.

With a sickening crack, the creature's grip faltered, and it fell back into the pit, shrieking in fury as it disappeared into the darkness below. Derek pulled

Rachel up onto the ledge, both of them collapsing in a heap, gasping for breath.

"Are you okay?" Derek panted, his face inches from hers, concern etched in every line.

Rachel nodded, though her ankle throbbed with pain. "Yeah... I think so," she whispered, trying to steady her breathing. "Let's... let's get out of here."

Claire and Eddie helped them to their feet, their faces pale but relieved. "We need to seal this place," Claire said urgently, glancing back toward the dark pit. "Those things... they won't stay down there forever."

Derek nodded, clutching the skull tightly to his chest. "There's an old mine entrance just up ahead," he said. "We can collapse it... seal them in."

They hurried down the tunnel, their footsteps echoing in the cold, silent air. The creatures' howls faded behind them, but the sense of urgency was still palpable. The mine shaft was just ahead, a crumbling archway of stone that led deeper into the mountain.

Derek spotted an old dynamite crate near the entrance, its wood splintered and rotting but still intact. "There!" he pointed. "We can use that to blow the entrance."

Eddie's eyes widened. "Are you serious?" he asked, his voice filled with apprehension. "That could bring the whole mountain down on us!"

Derek shook his head. "We don't have a choice," he replied firmly. "It's the only way to make sure those things don't follow us out."

Rachel moved to help him, her fingers moving quickly as she pulled out a stick of dynamite and checked the fuse. "Just be careful," she warned, glancing up at Derek. "We don't want to set this off too early."

They rigged the dynamite quickly, their movements swift and precise. Derek placed the explosives near the entrance, arranging them to ensure maximum impact. The air was thick with tension, every second stretching into an eternity.

Finally, Derek lit the fuse, the small flame hissing and crackling as it crept toward the explosives. "Run!" he shouted, grabbing Rachel's hand and pulling her back down the tunnel.

They sprinted, their feet pounding on the stone, the sound of the burning fuse growing louder behind them. Eddie and Claire were just ahead, their faces pale and drawn, their breaths coming in sharp, shallow gasps.

And then — Boom!

The explosion rocked the tunnel, a deafening roar that shook the ground beneath them. Rocks and debris rained down from above, the sound of crashing stone filling the air. Dust and smoke billowed through the tunnel, blinding them, choking them.

"Keep going!" Derek shouted, coughing as he pushed forward. "Don't stop!"

They stumbled through the dust and smoke, the tunnel shaking violently, stones and debris falling all around them. The sound of the collapse was deafening, a rumbling that seemed to go on forever.

Finally, they burst out into the open air, gasping for breath, their faces streaked with dirt and sweat.

The mountain groaned behind them, the sound of rocks shifting and settling filling the air.

They turned to look back, seeing the entrance to the mine covered in rubble, the dark, gaping maw now sealed shut, the creatures trapped within.

Derek held the skull tightly, his hands trembling. "We did it," he breathed, a mixture of relief and exhaustion in his voice. "We actually did it…"

Rachel leaned against him, her heart still racing. "But it's not over," she murmured, her eyes fixed on the skull. "We still have to bury it… in the right place… or this will never end."

Derek nodded, his face grim. "We head for the burial grounds," he said, determination in his voice. "And we finish this… once and for all."

And with that, they turned away from the mountain, the weight of the skull heavy in Derek's hands, the darkness still lingering around them, whispering its final, terrible secrets.

This content may violate our <u>usage policies</u>.

Did we get it wrong? Please tell us by giving this response a thumbs down.

Chapter 19: The Final Journey

The four of them—Derek, Rachel, Claire, and Eddie—made their way down the winding mountain path, each step feeling heavier than the last. The dense forest around them seemed to close in, its branches and leaves forming a tangled web overhead, blotting out the moonlight. The skull in Derek's hand felt like a dead weight, a cold and malevolent presence that seemed to pulse with its own dark energy. He couldn't shake the feeling that something—no, someone—was watching them.

"Are you sure we're going the right way?" Eddie asked, his voice barely a whisper. His usually confident tone was gone, replaced by a nervous tremor. His eyes darted around, searching the darkness for unseen threats.

Derek nodded, though his jaw was clenched tight. "Yeah," he said, forcing himself to sound certain. "The burial ground is on the other side of the ravine, near the old church ruins. It's the only place that fits the description in Annie's journal."

Rachel glanced over at him, her face illuminated by the faint glow of her flashlight. "You're sure this is where she was buried?" she pressed. "This has to be right... or everything we just did was for nothing."

Derek hesitated, then nodded again. "I'm sure," he

said, though doubt gnawed at the edges of his mind. The journal had been cryptic, its pages filled with half-mad ramblings and obscure references. But this was their only lead, their only chance to put an end to the terror of Headless Annie once and for all.

Claire walked beside Rachel, her hand gripping a small, leather-bound book she had found in the abandoned house—a Bible, its cover cracked and worn with age. "If this doesn't work," she murmured, glancing over at Derek, "what do we do then?"

Derek shook his head. "There's no 'if,' Claire," he said. "This has to work."

The tension between them hung heavy in the air, a palpable weight that seemed to press down on their shoulders. They all felt it—the unease, the creeping dread that had settled over them like a shroud. The forest was silent, too silent, as if even the animals knew to keep their distance. The wind rustled the leaves above, creating eerie whispers that sounded almost like voices, murmuring just out of earshot.

"We need to move faster," Derek urged, quickening his pace. "The longer we stay out here, the more danger we're in."

As they continued along the path, Rachel fell into step beside Derek. "Are you okay?" she asked quietly, her brow furrowed with concern. "You've been holding that skull for hours now... it can't be easy."

Derek sighed, his grip tightening around the bone. "It's... heavy," he admitted, his voice low. "Not just physically, but... it feels like it's alive, somehow. Like it's angry that we took it away from the cave."

Rachel nodded, understanding all too well. "You're doing great," she said, giving him a small, encouraging smile. "Just hang in there a little longer."

Derek managed a nod, but his expression was grim. He could feel the energy radiating from the skull, a malevolent force that seemed to seep into his very bones. He had to fight the urge to throw it away, to leave it behind and run as fast as he could in the opposite direction.

But he couldn't. Not yet. Not until they reached the burial ground.

As they walked, Rachel's mind drifted back to the events of the past few days—the terror they had faced, the lives they had almost lost. She thought of her sister, lost to the darkness of the mountain, and felt a surge of determination. They had to finish this. They had to bring peace to Headless Annie and all the souls trapped in this cursed place.

Eddie suddenly stopped, his eyes wide. "Did you hear that?" he whispered, his flashlight beam darting through the trees.

Claire paused beside him, her face pale. "Hear what?" she asked, though her voice was tense with

apprehension.

Eddie turned his head slowly, his ears straining. "Footsteps," he said, his voice barely more than a breath. "Coming from behind us... and getting closer."

They all froze, their breath catching in their throats. Derek felt a chill run down his spine as he listened intently, his senses on high alert. For a moment, there was nothing but the whisper of the wind and the distant rustle of leaves.

Then, faint but unmistakable, came the sound of footsteps crunching on the dry leaves—a slow, deliberate pace, as if whoever or whatever was following them wanted them to know they were there.

"Run," Derek whispered, his voice urgent. "Now!"

They broke into a sprint, the underbrush tearing at their clothes, branches whipping against their faces. The footsteps behind them quickened, the sound growing louder, closer, as if whatever was back there was gaining on them.

Rachel glanced over her shoulder, her heart pounding in her chest. She saw a figure in white— a pale, shadowy shape moving swiftly through the trees. Her breath hitched in her throat. "It's her," she gasped. "It's Annie!"

The ghost moved with an unnatural speed, gliding over the ground, her headless form somehow more terrifying in the shifting shadows of the forest. Her white dress was stained with mud and blood, her

movements jerky and unnatural. And even without a head, she seemed to stare directly at them, her presence exuding an aura of rage and sorrow.

"Keep running!" Derek shouted, his grip on the skull tightening, his legs burning with exertion. "Don't look back!"

They tore through the forest, their breaths coming in sharp gasps, their hearts hammering in their chests. The air was thick with fear, every sound amplified, every shadow a potential threat.

And then, up ahead, they saw it—the church ruins, silhouetted against the dark sky, its stone walls crumbling and overgrown with ivy. The burial ground lay just beyond it, the place they hoped would be the end of their nightmare.

"There!" Derek pointed, his voice hoarse with urgency. "We're almost there!"

But as they neared the church, the air grew colder, the temperature plummeting sharply, their breaths turning to mist in the icy air. A low, mournful wail filled the forest, a sound that seemed to come from everywhere and nowhere at once. It was a sound of despair, of longing, and it sent a chill through their very souls.

"She's trying to stop us," Claire gasped, clutching the Bible to her chest. "She doesn't want to be laid to rest."

Eddie's face was pale, his eyes wide with fear. "We have to keep going," he muttered, almost to himself. "We have to... we have to..."

They pushed forward, reaching the edge of the burial ground, a clearing filled with ancient tombstones, some broken and half-buried in the earth. Derek held up the skull, his hands trembling. "This is it," he said, his voice barely audible over the sound of the wind. "This is where it ends."

Rachel nodded, tears in her eyes. "Do it, Derek," she urged. "Finish it."

Derek took a deep breath, stepping forward into the center of the clearing. He could feel the cold seeping into his bones, the darkness pressing in around him. He held the skull high, his voice steady as he began to recite the words from the journal, the ancient incantation meant to lay Annie to rest.

But as he spoke, the wind picked up, a fierce, howling gale that whipped around them, tearing at their clothes and hair. The ground beneath their feet began to tremble, the tombstones rattling in their sockets.

And then, with a sound like shattering glass, a blinding light erupted from the skull, a beam of pure white energy that shot up into the sky, piercing the darkness. The light grew brighter, expanding outward, enveloping the entire clearing.

Annie's ghost screamed, a high, keening wail that echoed through the forest, her form flickering and wavering in the light. She reached out with clawed hands, her movements desperate, but the light pushed her back, driving her away.

"No!" Derek shouted over the roar of the wind. "You're not taking any more lives! This ends now!"

Rachel, Claire, and Eddie formed a circle around him, their hands clasped together, their faces determined. Claire began to recite a prayer, her voice strong and steady, and Rachel joined in, adding her own voice to the incantation.

The light grew even brighter, a blinding white that consumed everything. Annie's ghost screamed again, a sound of pure agony and rage. She clawed at the air, her form beginning to dissolve, to fade, as if she were being pulled apart by some unseen force.

And then, with one final, terrible scream, she was gone. The light dimmed, the wind died down, and the forest was silent once more.

Derek lowered the skull, his hands shaking. "Is it over?" he asked, his voice barely a whisper.

Rachel nodded, tears streaming down her face. "I think so," she said, her voice thick with emotion. "I think... we did it."

The four of them stood there, breathing hard, their hearts still racing, the adrenaline slowly draining from their veins. The air was still cold, but there was a new sense of peace, a calmness that hadn't been there before.

"Let's bury it," Derek

"Let's bury it," Derek repeated, more firmly this time, his voice cutting through the silence.

He moved to the center of the clearing, where the light had erupted moments ago. The earth there seemed softer, almost inviting. Rachel handed him the small shovel they had brought, her hands still trembling. Without a word, Derek began to dig, the blade sinking easily into the loose dirt.

As he worked, the others kept watch, their eyes scanning the shadows that surrounded the clearing. Claire, still clutching the Bible, whispered a prayer under her breath, asking for protection and guidance. Eddie, standing a few feet away, wiped the sweat from his brow, his body still humming with the residual fear and adrenaline. He glanced over at Rachel, who was staring intently at Derek, her face a mixture of hope and dread.

"Are you sure this will be enough?" Eddie asked, his voice hushed.

Rachel didn't take her eyes off Derek. "It has to be," she said quietly. "If we've read the journal right, returning her remains to the earth, to her rightful grave, should finally put her spirit to rest."

Derek paused for a moment, wiping his forehead with the back of his hand. The hole was deep enough now—about three feet down, the soil rich and dark. He took a deep breath and placed the skull carefully into the hole, feeling a shiver run down his spine as it settled into the earth.

"Say the words, Rachel," Derek said, stepping back.

Rachel nodded, her hands shaking as she held up

the journal. Her voice was steady as she began to read the final incantation. It was an old prayer, a mix of English and Latin, words meant to cleanse and consecrate the ground. Her voice grew stronger with each line, the power of the words building with a force that seemed to resonate through the earth itself.

As she spoke, the air around them seemed to grow thicker, heavier. The light of the moon dimmed, the shadows lengthening. Claire and Eddie drew closer to each other, their eyes darting around nervously. Derek could feel the energy around them shift, a low hum vibrating in the very core of his being.

Rachel continued, her voice unwavering. "Rest now, Annie... find your peace in the soil of your home. Let the earth cradle you, let the light guide you... let your spirit find the release it has long sought."

The ground seemed to pulse, the soil around the skull shifting and moving as if being pulled by some unseen force. Derek stepped forward, beginning to cover the skull with dirt, his movements careful, almost reverent. Each shovelful felt like a small weight being lifted from his shoulders, the burden of the night slowly easing with each scoop.

But just as the last bit of dirt fell over the skull, the earth shuddered violently, a tremor that rippled through the clearing, sending them all stumbling. A cold, eerie wind whipped through the trees,

howling like a chorus of mournful voices.

Derek looked around, panic flashing in his eyes. "What's happening?" he shouted over the wind.

Rachel's heart pounded in her chest. "I don't know!" she replied, struggling to keep her footing. "I did everything right, I... I think..."

Suddenly, a deep, guttural moan emanated from beneath the ground, a sound that seemed to vibrate through the earth itself. The ground where they had buried the skull began to crack, fissures spreading out in all directions like spiderwebs. A foul smell filled the air, a mix of decay and sulfur, making them all gag.

"No... no!" Claire cried, clutching the Bible to her chest. "It's not working, it's—"

Before she could finish, the earth erupted in a blinding flash of light. A figure began to rise from the ground—a translucent, shimmering form that slowly took shape. It was Annie. But this time, she was whole. She had a head, her long dark hair flowing around her face like a veil. Her eyes were closed, her expression serene... almost peaceful.

For a moment, no one moved, their eyes locked on the ghostly figure hovering above the ground.

Then Annie's eyes snapped open. They were filled with tears, and she looked directly at them, her gaze piercing, a mixture of sorrow and gratitude.

"Thank you..." Her voice was soft, barely more than a whisper, but it echoed through the clearing, filling their ears and minds.

Rachel stepped forward, her heart racing. "Is it... is it over? Are you... free?"

Annie nodded slowly, her face softening, her spectral form beginning to fade. "I was never lost," she murmured. "Only waiting... for someone to understand."

Her words hung in the air, heavy with meaning. The wind began to die down, the light around them softening, and the earth seemed to settle beneath their feet.

"Go now," Annie whispered, her voice growing fainter. "Leave this place... and do not look back."

And with that, her form dissolved completely, a soft glow spreading out, then dissipating into the night like a mist caught in the morning sun.

The forest fell silent. The wind stopped, the air warming around them. The oppressive feeling lifted, replaced by a calm, almost serene stillness. They stood there, breathing hard, their hearts slowly calming.

"Is it really over?" Eddie finally asked, his voice hushed.

Derek nodded, a slow smile spreading across his face. "I think so," he said, feeling a weight lift from his chest. "I think... we did it."

Rachel let out a shaky breath, tears streaming down her face. "We did," she whispered, a smile breaking through her tears. "We really did."

Claire sank to her knees, still clutching the Bible, her eyes wide with disbelief and relief. "Thank God," she breathed. "Thank God..."

They stood there for a moment longer, letting the reality of what had just happened settle in. Then, slowly, they began to make their way back down the path, the darkness of the forest now feeling less threatening, less oppressive.

Behind them, in the clearing, the soil seemed to settle into place, the last of the fissures closing, the earth finally at peace.

And as they walked, the night air felt warmer, more welcoming. The fog that had clung to the mountain for so long seemed to lift, revealing the stars above, twinkling brightly in the clear night sky. The silence was now peaceful, the forest alive with the soft sounds of nature reclaiming its own.

Rachel glanced back one last time, a small smile on her lips. "Goodbye, Annie," she whispered. "Rest now... and thank you."

They continued down the path, the weight of the skull gone, the darkness behind them no longer filled with fear but with the quiet peace of the mountain finally laid to rest.

CHAPTER 20: "THE FINAL RECKONING"

The forest was eerily quiet as they made their way down the narrow path, their footsteps crunching against the dry leaves and twigs. The mountain, now shrouded in a different kind of silence, felt almost serene. Yet there was a lingering tension in

the air, a subtle hum that pressed on their senses like a distant whisper they couldn't quite hear. Rachel could still feel the energy buzzing beneath her skin, a sensation that kept her nerves taut as a bowstring.

"We should hurry," Derek urged, his voice breaking the fragile calm. He moved quickly, his eyes darting around, scanning the shadows.

Despite Annie's peaceful departure, he couldn't shake the feeling that something wasn't right. Something felt... incomplete.

Rachel nodded, picking up her pace, though her heart was still racing with the adrenaline of what they'd just experienced. She felt Eddie's hand on her shoulder, a reassuring squeeze, but when she looked back at him, his face was still pale, his brow furrowed with concern.

"What is it?" she asked.

Eddie shook his head slowly. "I don't know... it just feels like it's not over, you know?"

Claire, who had been trailing behind, looked up sharply, her eyes wide. "You felt that too?" she whispered, clutching the Bible tighter to her chest. "Like... like something's still here?"

They all stopped, exchanging uneasy glances. The forest around them seemed to grow darker, the shadows lengthening as if something unseen was drawing closer.

"We buried the skull, performed the ritual... what else could there be?" Derek asked, his voice tinged

with frustration.

Rachel's mind raced, replaying the events of the night over and over. "Maybe... maybe we missed something," she murmured, turning the pages of the journal in her hands. The old, weathered book seemed to pulse with a life of its own, the ink almost shifting on the page.

"What do you mean?" Claire asked, a tremor in her voice.

"Annie's last words," Rachel whispered. "She said she was 'never lost... only waiting for someone to understand.' But what did she mean by that?"

Derek's eyes narrowed. "Maybe she wasn't talking about just the skull... maybe there's something else. Something more..."

As if in response, a cold gust of wind swept through the trees, sending a shiver down their spines. The leaves rustled and swirled around them, whispering secrets they couldn't quite catch.

Eddie swallowed hard, his eyes scanning the darkened tree-line. "What if we didn't just set her free... but awakened something else?"

Before anyone could respond, the ground beneath them rumbled, a low, ominous growl that seemed to rise from deep within the earth. The trees around them creaked and groaned, their branches swaying as if caught in an invisible current.

"We need to get out of here," Claire said urgently, her voice tight with fear.

Rachel nodded, tucking the journal under her arm. "Let's go... but keep your eyes open."

They resumed their descent, moving faster now, their senses on high alert. The forest seemed to press in around them, the darkness thickening like a living thing. Every snap of a twig, every rustle of leaves sent their hearts racing.

As they rounded a bend in the path, they saw it—a faint light flickering through the trees, just ahead. It was soft and golden, like a lantern swinging in the wind.

"Who else would be out here?" Derek muttered, his grip tightening on the shovel he still carried.

Rachel's heart skipped a beat. "Maybe... maybe it's just someone else. Another group of campers..."

But as they drew closer, the light seemed to dance and flicker, moving erratically, as if it were alive. And then they heard it—a faint, mournful wail that sent chills down their spines. The sound was distant but unmistakable, like a cry of anguish echoing through the woods.

"Annie?" Claire whispered, her voice trembling.

"No," Rachel replied, her eyes wide with realization. "Not Annie... but something... something connected to her."

The light flickered again, moving faster now, darting between the trees. Rachel felt a sudden urge to follow it, her feet moving almost on their own. She heard Derek calling her name, but his

voice seemed distant, muffled by the strange fog that began to settle over the path.

"Rachel, wait!" Eddie shouted, grabbing her arm.

But Rachel felt a pull, a compulsion deep within her that she couldn't ignore. "I have to see..." she whispered, her voice hollow, her eyes fixed on the dancing light. "I have to understand..."

The light flickered again, and suddenly, she was running, her feet pounding against the forest floor. She could hear the others calling after her, their voices tinged with panic, but they sounded miles away. She felt the fog thickening around her, swallowing the trees, the path, everything but the light ahead.

She ran until she burst into a small clearing, panting, her heart hammering in her chest. The light hovered in the center, flickering gently. And then she saw her.

Annie.

Not the headless, vengeful spirit they had seen before, but a young woman, whole and radiant, her hair flowing in the soft light, her eyes filled with sadness.

Rachel froze, unable to speak, her breath catching in her throat. Annie stared at her, and for a moment, Rachel saw a flicker of recognition in her eyes.

"You came..." Annie's voice was soft, almost a sigh. "But you still don't understand."

Rachel swallowed, finding her voice. "What... what don't I understand?"

Annie's face twisted in sorrow. "My story... my pain... was never just mine. It's tied to this place, to those who suffered before me... and those who will suffer after."

Rachel felt a chill run down her spine. "But... we buried you. We did the ritual. We tried to set you free!"

Annie shook her head slowly, her eyes filled with tears. "You set me free... but the darkness here... it's deeper than you know. It's older. It's always been here, waiting... feeding on the lost, the broken."

Rachel's heart pounded in her chest. "What do you mean? What are you saying?"

Annie stepped closer, her form beginning to fade. "The curse... it's not just mine. It belongs to this place... to the mountain. And it's hungry, Rachel... it's always hungry."

And with that, Annie vanished, the light winking out, leaving Rachel alone in the dark.

"Rachel!" Derek's voice pierced the darkness, and she turned to see him rushing into the clearing, followed by Eddie and Claire. "What happened? Are you okay?"

Rachel blinked, still in shock. "She... she was here. Annie... she said... it's not just her. It's the mountain... it's... it's hungry."

Eddie looked around, his face pale. "Then... what did we do? Did we just... wake it up?"

Claire clutched the Bible to her chest, her voice trembling. "We need to leave. Now."

But as they turned to go, the ground trembled again, a deep, resonant thrum that seemed to come from all around them. The trees groaned and shifted, the fog thickening once more, swirling around them like a living thing.

And then they heard it—a deep, guttural laugh that seemed to echo from the very depths of the earth, a sound filled with malice and hunger.

Rachel felt a cold dread wash over her. "We... we need to run," she whispered, her voice barely more than a breath.

They took off, running as fast as they could, the laughter following them, growing louder, closer. The fog thickened, swallowing the path, the trees, everything around them.

As they ran, Rachel felt something brush against her arm, a cold, clammy touch that made her scream. She glanced back and saw a shadowy figure reaching out from the fog, its eyes glowing with an unnatural light.

"Go, go!" Derek shouted, pushing her forward, his face a mask of fear.

They ran faster, their breaths coming in ragged gasps, their hearts pounding in their chests. The fog seemed to close in around them, the laughter growing louder, more menacing. The path ahead

was barely visible, a narrow strip of light in the encroaching darkness.

Suddenly, they burst out of the fog and into the parking lot where their car was waiting. They scrambled inside, slamming the doors shut, their breaths coming in panicked bursts.

"Drive, Derek!" Rachel shouted, her voice hoarse.

Derek fumbled with the keys, his hands shaking. The engine roared to life, and he floored the gas, the tires screeching as they sped down the mountain road.

Behind them, in the rearview mirror, Rachel saw the fog rolling down the hillside, a dark, creeping mass that seemed to follow them, hungry and relentless.

As they raced down the mountain, she felt a chill run down her spine, a sense of dread that wouldn't leave. She glanced at the journal in her lap, the old pages rustling in the wind.

They had freed Annie, but they had awakened something far worse. Something that wouldn't rest. Something that was always waiting, always hungry.

As they reached the bottom of the mountain, the fog seemed to stop, hovering at the edge of the road like a living thing. But Rachel knew it wouldn't stay there forever. It was only a matter of time before it reached out again... before it found another soul to claim.

Derek glanced at her, his face pale and drawn.

"What do we do now?" he asked, his voice barely a whisper.

Rachel stared ahead, her mind racing. "We find out what it wants," she said slowly. "And we stop it... whatever it takes."

Eddie nodded, his face set with determination. "We've come this far... we can't turn back now."

Claire clutched the Bible tightly, her knuckles white. "We need to be ready... because whatever is out there... it's coming for us."

Rachel nodded, her eyes narrowing. "Then we'll be ready," she said, her voice filled with resolve. "Because this isn't over. Not by a long shot."

And as they drove away, the fog began to move again, creeping slowly down the mountain, a dark shadow that would never stop... until it found what it was looking for.

The True Story of Headless Annie on Black Mountain

For decades, the ghost of Headless Annie has haunted the winding,

fog-covered roads of Black Mountain in Harlan, Kentucky. Locals

speak of a woman dressed in white, her head missing, who

appears on dark,misty nights to those unfortunate enough to cross

her path. The stories, passed down through generations,

are chillingly consistent: a headless figure emerging from the shadows,

her presence felt long before she is seen, and the sudden disappearance

of those who encounter her. This book, "Headless Annie: is a work of

fiction, but it draws inspiration from numerous real-life accounts of

those who claim to have encountered Headless Annie.